Chiclet Gomez

Chiclet Gomez

Dorothy O'Connell

Deneau & Greenberg
Ottawa

DEDICATION

This book is for Aline and Carol and Diana and Gaye and Irene and Lila and Mary and Ruth and for all the other tough ladies who live in public housing . . .
And for the Prime Minister . . .
And the Mayor . . .
And the Housing Authority . . .
And the bigots, without whose loyal opposition none of this could have come to pass . . .
And for all my patient family . . .
And for the CBC who gave me a chance to try it out . . .
And for my loving and supportive husband . . .
Hell, this book is for everybody.

CONTENTS

THE FAT FARM FIASCO

I was sitting in my writer's chair, wearing the hat from which I derive my inspiration, when there was a knock on the door, and in bounced Chiclet. Chiclet's my neighbour.

Perhaps I should note here that I'm going to try and be very conscientious in this report and try to put down everything just as it is. Or was. Where was I? Oh yes, in bounced Chiclet.

"It's May!" she burbled. "Come on, Tillie! Time for exercise and diet. Let's go. Let's go - march!"

I was somewhat taken aback. About the only thing I like less than exercise is bingo. Especially group exercise. This is where some lady almost as overweight as you are turns up in a pair of bulgy black tights and jollies you along as you all sweat and grunt together. She always calls you "girls". I haven't been a girl since sometime in the nineteen-fifties. But it's no good arguing with Chiclet. I took off my pith helmet and followed her out the door.

Looking back, I don't think I could have prevented any of what happened. Call it fate, or kismet, or something. I figure it was inevitable. Anything that Chiclet organizes goes its own inexorable way.

You may wonder how I got involved with Chiclet, and why I don't stay out of her way. When Chiclet Gomez first moved into our public housing project, she was carving herself out a career as a child bride. At that point, we didn't have much in common — I was an old lady of twenty-eight, and she was a mere infant of nineteen. However, over the years, we've discovered that we have two things in common — a desire to make some money, and a distinct disinclination to attain this goal by making other people's bathrooms sparkle. We tried our separate ways at first, with no noticeable success or failure. Once we started putting our heads together though, something happened.

I'm separated, and I used to go over to Chiclet's to hash over new schemes to make a million. Her husband claimed I was a bad influence on her. This was nonsense, of course. How could a middle-aged mother be a bad influence on the girl who used to turn into a gorilla on the carnie circuit? (I could tell you how it's done, but that's a long story; suffice it to say that she couldn't do it *at will* which is the only way I'd enjoy it.)

Anyway, when Chiclet decided we were going into the Fat Farm business, I thought it was worth a try. At this point we had already tried candied flowers (this turned out to be a bit premature, and midnight raids on the neighbours' flower boxes in search of something edible did not make us popular), collaborating on an erotic novel (Chiclet's husband caught us coming out of a porno store where we had been trying to do research - it didn't work anyway, because we didn't have the money for the deposit), making souvenirs for government officials who tour the project from time to time (now that was a bust - everybody was angry - the neighbours have this mad compulsion to be respectable, and it appears to be shared by the Housing Authority),

2

and our TV show. That's when Chiclet's husband finally left. High time, too. Anyway, the only thing wrong with the TV show was that it was on a community channel and didn't pay. It certainly got us a fair amount of fame. Or notoriety. It was also indirectly responsible for the downfall of the Fat Farm.

The FF started out as the best plan yet. All the straight-arrow ladies in the community decided we had finally reformed. They all came out. We had wall-to-wall fat. You might say we had cornered the fat market in the project. We charged them each a dollar for the course. Chiclet had it all worked out. Fancy diets are too expensive for people in our income bracket, so she had decided the method to use was exercise, laxatives, and starvation. Half of the profits were poured into buying a laxative from the drugstore which came with vitamin pills, so no one would actually starve. Chiclet's scales were generally out about two pounds in her favour, so this gave encouragement. We put the laxative into unsweetened grapefruit juice, and doled it out twice a day when we exercised. Morning and evening, things were really starting to hum. This could have been IT, if it hadn't been for Fat Freddy Hernandez.

Fat Freddie is Chiclet's husband's cousin, and his spy. The only reason Chiclet lets him come around is, if she didn't, King Kong would probably turn up himself. He's got this dream that someday Chiclet will realize she needs him, and beg him to come back. He's not above stacking the odds a little, either.

I should say right here that Chiclet and I are not against men. We just don't care for the institution of marriage. Institution is the word all right. Any other custom that took a young girl with a lot of life in her and turned her into a worn-out drudge by the time she was twenty-five would be called slavery. But we are not manhaters.

The walls were vibrating to the sound of the Rolling

Stones and acres of fat being slammed on the floor, which is why whenever it was that Fat Freddie got into the Community Centre, he did it without anybody being the wiser.

When we all trooped into the kitchen for our grapefruit juice plus, we were a pretty bedraggled lot. For three weeks we had been working at shrinking down to nothing, and none of us was in the mood for any light frivolity. Our days had turned into a nightmare of exercise, starvation, dreams of forbidden food, and treks to the bathroom. We were as empty as kettledrums, and as snarly as snares. Any fool but Freddie would have taken one good look and fled. Freddie may have weighed as much as any two of us, but we had him outnumbered.

Freddie started razzing us as we were lining up for our shot.

"So, Dolores, you've joined the ranks of Women's Lib. When are you throwing out your old man? What're you girls training for, anyway?"

We huddled collectively near the punch bowl and tried to ignore him. This was not easy, as Freddie has one of those voices that scrapes on your nerves even if he's trying to be pleasant. Suddenly I realized I was on my third glass of grapefruit juice. I paled as I realized what the next day would hold in store for me. Then I got angry. I told Freddie to get out or I would throw him out.

"You tell him, Tillie."

"Yeah, throw him out!"

The cheers from the ladies, plus my unaccustomed bravery, suddenly registered. We had all had three glasses or so. Cautiously I sipped. It tasted good. Good? We had all gagged on the stuff up to now. It could only mean one thing. Freddie had spiked the juice.

"Get him out of here before there's a riot, " I hissed to Chiclet, "and throw out the juice."

"Never mind him," she said. "Our Fat Farm is going to make money. This stuff I put together is good."

"That's the trouble. It's too good. Freddie spiked it. We've got a bunch of smashed teetotallers on our hands."

That's when the riot started. The combination of booze, starvation, regular doses of laxative, and Fat Freddie was deadly. We managed to get rid of Freddie, but we still had a problem. The neighbours couldn't go home drunk. We were in big trouble. Again.

I started making a big pot of black coffee, and Chiclet decided to give them a pep talk. All she wanted to do was to cheer them up a little, and prepare them for trouble from their husbands, but I guess they were too receptive.

"Ladies! How often have you come home drunk?"

"Never!" Murmurs of agreement.

"How often has your husband come home drunk?"
Loud murmurs, gradually building into a crescendo.

"We've all heard about how disgusting drunken women are, right? How about drunken men?"

"Right!"

"Sisters! Why should your husbands have rights you can't enjoy? Why shouldn't you have a few drinks with your friends? Equal rights for women!"

"RIGHT ON!"

Out the door they poured, encouraged, exhorted by each other. Mrs. Grocholski went right home and beat the daylights out of her husband. He deserved it. He'd been knocking her around every Friday for at least seven years. I know, because I live next door.

Mrs. Pettigrew and Georgia Wiseman suddenly decided they were joining Women's Lib. They wriggled out of their bras (you know how you can wiggle out without removing another stitch? — I mean, they were still *decent*) and ran through the back of the project,

5

trailing them behind, fluttering in the breeze. Then they set them on fire.

The men came out and laughed. All except Mr. Wiseman and Mr. Pettigrew. They were furious.

"Georgia! Stop that! What do you think you're doing?"

"Up with women! Down with men!"

"Dolores! Get in the house! Right now!"

"Try and make me! I dare you!"

Up surged the ladies.

"Leave them alone, you billies!"

Three more ladies added their bras to the fire. Their husbands stopped laughing.

"What the Hell's the matter with your wife, Pettigrew? Do you see what she's got my old lady doing?"

"My wife! It's your wife. She's bombed out of her tree."

"She must be sick. She never..."

"Face facts, Ralph. She's hammered."

"You can't talk about my wife like that!"

Pow! Suddenly everybody was fighting. Fists and curses were flung with abandon. Women were laughing and screaming. It was no place for a lady, so I beat a hasty retreat, dragging Chiclet with me. We did not escape unscathed. Somebody stepped on her foot, and I got an elbow in the eye. Chiclet wanted to make somebody pay for these indignities, she didn't care who, but I got here safely to my house before the paddy wagon and the fire engine arrived. My kids wanted to go out and watch, but I wouldn't let them. I think it's vulgar to go out and watch a fight.

That was yesterday. I haven't gone out today. For one thing, as they say in westerns, "It's quiet out there. Too quiet." For another, I need to stay near the ice for my eye, and near the bathroom for other reasons. I think maybe my kids are right. It is time to grow up and settle

6

down. They keep telling me they want an ordinary mother, not the oldest hippie in the project. They're right. I'm turning over a new leaf. I may even hang up my pith helmet.

> *My last fling*
> *Has been flung;*
> *My last bell*
> *Has been rung;*
> *My last song*
> *Has been sung;*
> *My last dog*
> *Has been hung;*
> *My last bang*
> *Has been bung;*
> *Now I'm only half alive —*
> *Tomorrow I turn thirty-five.*

Chiclet just came to the door. She says the newsmen are here to interview us about the riot. Great press coverage. She thinks one of us should run for mayor. The other one can be campaign manager. She's right. This could be our big chance. Thirty-five is a good age for a mayor.

AMONG MY SOUVENIRS

Whenever Chiclet has an idea, it is like someone tosses a pebble into a puddle. The ripples spread outward, and everybody gets wet. Some people get in over their heads, some just wet their toes, and some plunge in with gusto. I tend to get up to my waist and panic.

The trouble is, Chiclet is full of ideas. I find myself all wet far too often for my own comfort, but then how important is comfort really? I must like being in the middle of a crisis, or they wouldn't keep happening to me. Every time Chiclet has one of her great ideas, I can think of all kinds of rational reasons for going along with her. What I can't figure out is everyone else's reasons.

Any idea Chiclet has is always tried out on a few people first. Linda Cunningham thinks Chiclet is wonderful, so she'll agree to anything Chiclet suggests, and work her head off, besides. This is not to say that Linda is stupid. Chiclet has helped Linda out of a lot of fixes, and Linda trusts her implicitly. I always have reservations, but I get caught up in the excitement of planning, and although I know trouble is sure to follow,

8

I also know that nothing else half as exciting as one of Chiclet's inspirations is going to come my way, so I usually agree, even if I argue a lot first. Edna generally thinks it's a lousy idea. The only trouble is, she is not an original thinker, so generally she decides we might as well try, even if it's bound to fail. I think that must be why her hair is always in curlers. She's so sure that it won't work, she never takes them out to see if it has. Mrs. Grocholski knows very well that her husband hates her to have anything to do with Chiclet or me. This is her one act of rebellion, even though all she does is come to the meeting and worry about her husband finding out she's there. Poison Ivy always comes in the hope that a real catastrophe will happen that she can tell everybody about, and Georgia Wiseman comes to see if there's any chance that someone will notice how gorgeous she is and how much weight she's lost, and in case there will be any men involved.

Every month there is a meeting at somebody's house, to celebrate or mourn the last idea, and to plan the next one. First we spend an hour or so drinking tea and coffee, eating cookies, and talking about What Went Wrong. Something always did. We also discuss What Did Not Go Wrong, and to give Chiclet credit, there's usually something to offer here, too. Georgia usually spends this time telling everyone how many people told her how gorgeous she is, and how much weight she lost. Poison Ivy has usually got a new rumour about some perfectly respectable person who she always suspected of being too good to be true. Last time she was sure the Mayor had made a pass at Linda, although Linda says he just spilled his drink on her, and was trying to mop it up. This put Georgia's nose out of joint, as she figures if anyone is going to get a pass made at them, it should be her.

"Ladies. The Bake Sale made a total of thirty-five dollars after expenses. This will help to get our

Community Centre off the ground. I want to thank you all for the effort you put into it. Now, what are our suggestions for this month?"

"Wait a minute, Chiclet. What expenses?"

"I'm glad you asked, Edna. As you know, we had to split the profits with Father Florian, and he had the coffee concession. So, actually, we made a profit of seventy dollars. Then there were the expenses for cleaning Linda's dress, cleaning the hall after the Bun Fight, and refilling the fire extinguishers. Actually, we took in a lot of money. We just didn't get to keep much of it."

"You didn't have to pay for my dress, Chiclet."

"Don't be silly, Linda. Acts of Mayor fall under the same section as Acts of God. As far as dry cleaning goes, anyway."

"Is Father Florian still threatening to sue us?"

"Nope. I told him, you can't get blood from a turnip. Anyway, he realizes it was all an accident. But it does mean we can't use the hall. I'm just as glad. It was too expensive anyway."

The trouble is, we didn't have anywhere else to use for any of our plans. The local high school didn't want any part of us, and our houses were certainly too small to hold any number of people. Even with just the seven of us in Chiclet's kitchen, I wasn't really in the kitchen. I was sitting on the floor in the hall, with my feet in the living room.

"What about outside? A beauty contest would be nice outside."

Even without looking, I knew it was Georgia. Georgia always suggests a beauty contest. I don't think she really wants one, because it might bring in some outside competition. She just likes to rub it in that of seven of us she is the only one in any shape to enter.

After the usual freezing silence, Chiclet said she was thinking of a garage sale.

"But we don't have garages. We don't even have basements. How can we have a garage sale?"

"Don't be a defeatist, Tillie. Did you ever see a white elephant at a White Elephant sale?"

She had me there.

"Look. We all have junk we'd love to get rid of. Right? But we can't afford to have it hauled away. So, instead of paying someone to take it off our hands, we'll let them pay us."

"But our junk isn't even second hand. Our junk is fourth or fifth hand. Who'd want it?"

"That's easy. We'll auction it off. People will buy anything if they think they're getting it cheap. We'll call it a penny auction. I can see it now... Take a chance for just pennies. You may find a priceless antique!"

Linda loved it. Edna hated it. She was sure it was going to rain. I was sort of intrigued — there was this motheaten deer's head that had been kicking around the house for years that I wanted to get rid of.

It was settled. We would have the garage sale in the parking lot of the project in two weeks. Chiclet decided that she would be responsible for getting permission to use the parking lot. She phoned the manager of the Housing Authority and asked him if he would be the auctioneer. This was taking a chance, because Chiclet desperately wanted to be the auctioneer. However, he reacted just the way she thought he would. He panicked at the thought of exposure to all us public housing tenants, and when she let him off the hook, he was more than glad to give permission to use the parking lot.

We started to round up junk. For once, the other neighbours were interested in the idea. Even Mr. Grocholski admitted it was a good idea. He volunteered his car. It had been sitting in the parking lot so long the Housing Authority had said they were going to tow it away, and make him pay the charges. It was hard to tell how they knew it was a car. It resembled a large lump of rust.

11

The day of the big garage sale was clear and warm. Chiclet, Linda and I were out at dawn, lugging all the junk we'd collected. Having no place to store it, we had used our houses, and I hadn't been able to find a place to sit down in my own house for days. Everywhere you looked there were discarded potties, and dolls without arms, and solitary salt shakers, and chairs without legs, and teapots without spouts, and lids without pots.

We had amassed a mountain of junk. We decided to put it into lots. Lot one was fifty-three salt and pepper shakers. Lot two was assorted toys, and so on.

Early in the day, people began to turn up in trickles. Among the first trickles were King Kong and Fat Freddy.

"Look out. Here comes trouble."

We had no actual proof that Freddie had thrown the first bun in the Big Bun Fight, and it may not have been King Kong who stopped it with the fire hose, but we knew from past experience that they only attended if they thought there was something they could do to ruin the whole thing.

"Ladies and Gentlemen, if you will cast your eyes on this beautiful lamp which I am going to auction off, you will see that it is a real rarity—a trilight with only one socket. What am I bid for this gem? You, sir, in the first row—was that a gleam of interest? How about a nickel? We have a nickel, how about a dime? One thin dime, ladies and gentlemen, and this unique object can be yours..."

While Chiclet was auctioneering, I tried to work my way unobtrusively closer to King Kong and Freddie. There was quite a mob, so I felt they wouldn't notice me. So far, our auction looked pretty good. For a change, some money was going to come in from people other than the rest of the tenants in the project. I noticed the local alderman in the crowd, not bidding at the moment, but the day was still young, and we were saving the quality items till later.

One of these was our communal fox fur. Every woman in the project had worn it at least once, so it was time to get a new one. I don't remember where it originally came from, but it had had a varied existence in the project. It had attended weddings, funerals, baptisms, football games, bingos, graduations, bean suppers, highland balls, and God knows what else. Like the old story of the three old women with only one ear, one eye and one tooth between them, we had gathered together a very respectable outfit which was available when anyone had to go anywhere. There was The Fur, The Purse (a superannuated evening bag), and The Shoes. Other clothes were also interchanged, but tended to remain with their original (as far as the project went anyhow) owners. I had a dress that Chiclet, Georgia and I had all worn, but the others were too small for it, and Georgia had a pant suit that we all tried to get into, and Chiclet had a coat for good occasions.

The reason for getting rid of The Fur, and not the others, was that we had all worn it to the Housing Authority on different occasions. Usually, we kept our outings separate enough so that nobody saw more than one of us in The Outfit, but we had goofed. Still, it was sad to see it going. By the time I had finished these melancholy reflections, I was standing behind Fat Freddy and King Kong.

"Have they come to it yet? How much longer? I can't wait to see their faces..."

There was something in the air, all right. A definite hint of skunk. But what were they waiting for? It sounded like a booby trap. Was something going to explode? How to warn Chiclet?

Linda was up at the front, doing the running between audience and auctioneer, collecting the money and giving out the purchases. Georgia was also hanging around, hoping to model some of the clothing. I was supposed to be the shill, bidding on the things nobody else would start off. I had already fallen down on the job, and the odd salt and pepper shakers hadn't got a single bid. But wasn't this more important?

I decided to try and get around behind the platform, where the bulk of the junk was waiting to be sold. I didn't know where to begin. There was still a mountain of odd objects, precariously balanced. It would have to be small, whatever I was looking for, and easily hidden. Would it tick? Was that really a clock? I decided it was, and kept on looking. Some people throw away stuff that looks really good. A silver cocktail shaker! And a tea service with all the pieces!! Hmm... Nothing in the sugar bowl. Half of a bikini...three packages of cucumber bath powder...a peach coloured transparent nightgown obviously designed for a hippopotamus, with a note saying "never worn"...oh what was the use? I didn't even know what I was looking for.

I looked out at the crowd. There was Father Florian, bidding on a fruit bowl with ugly excrescences down the sides, supposedly representing grapes. What on earth could he want with that? Fat Freddie and King Kong were still there, smirking. I had to find it, whatever it was. I started to move faster. There was a peculiar parcel in that wastebasket...no. Just a neatly wrapped apple core. Aha! The deerhead! No, no openings. Wait. What was that peculiar lump in the cushion that said "Souvenir of Niagara Falls"? And what was the humming? I put my hand up the back of the cushion. Ow! I stuck myself with a needle. Ow! Another? Wasps!

I grabbed the cushion and headed for my laundry room. On the way, several managed to sting me, and my hops and leaps were interpreted as bids by an overeager Chiclet, who managed to sell me, I found out later, the nightgown, a set of scales that didn't work, and, of course, the cushion, which was lying drowned in my sink.

The role of heroine is not an easy one. Until they found out what had happened, everybody was mad at me for running out on the auction. Poison Ivy had spread a rumour that I had found a wad of money in the cushion and had run off with it, and the original owners wanted a cut, along with everybody else. Just the same, Chiclet was great, after she discovered what had happened. She made a big thing out of it, and everybody came over to inspect my stings. I sat on a cushion in my living room, holding court, covered in teabags. Teabags are Chiclet's favorite remedy for anything.

"What happened to the deerhead?"

"Oh, nobody wanted it."

"I'm not still stuck with it, am I?"

"Oh, no. Chiclet stuck a red rubber nose on it, and said it was Rudolph and Mr. Grocholski bought it. He's going to put it on his lawn at Christmas, and upset all the kids, with a sign that says *Santa can't make it this year*."

"What happened to Freddie and King Kong?"

"Oh, they hung around, and finally bought the salt and pepper shakers."

We made quite a bit of money, and we didn't have any expenses, but I still don't know why King Kong bought all those salt and pepper shakers, or what Father Florian is going to do with that fruit bowl, or where I'm going to put everything I ended up with, although Chiclet is all for having another auction just as soon as we get enough junk together.

If she does, she can hold it without me. Once bitten, twice shy, as they say. But I would like to get rid of that nightgown, and the scales, and one waterlogged Souvenir of Niagara Falls.

15

OF AGONIZING AND ORGANIZING

Chiclet wanted to have a meeting. It was the annual crack-down-on-the-tenants-and-show-them-who's-boss time of year, when the Housing Authority would decide we were getting uppity. Uppity was when you got a notice saying if you didn't pay off what you owed them in three days you'd be evicted, and instead of phoning them up like Chiclet would, and telling them off, you froze with fright and did nothing.

The trouble is, most of us are alone except for our children, and we aren't used to having traumatic decisions thrust on us like that. A lot of us don't even know what to do when our husbands desert us, even if we want them to. Lots of us sleep with a night light. We are the bold, bad, public housing tenants - the ones who, according to certain city officials, spend all our time breeding crime.

It was time, Chiclet thought, to show us that we were made of sterner stuff than we thought. So we sent a notice out to all the projects saying that we were going to have a meeting. We would form a group to raise our

16

consciousness and give us confidence in ourselves as people, and then we could all help those neighbours who hadn't advanced that far yet. It sounded fine. Of course I have discovered during the years that I've been Chiclet's friend that just because something sounds good at the time, it doesn't mean an automatic success. You'd think I would have become cynical by this time, but Chiclet always could get me enthusiastic.

One drawback to our plan was that we didn't yet have a meeting place. Chiclet and I went to see Father Florian.

"If it's about bingo," he said, "we get half the profits, and a cut on the soft drinks and chip sales, and..."

"It's not about bingo, Father," Chiclet said coolly. I was reeling in shock. Having been brought up a devout agnostic, I naturally had an exaggerated respect for Men of the Cloth, and this secular viewpoint was an eye-opener.

"It's about your hall, Father. We want to have a meeting, and we'd like to use it."

"What kind of meeting? A bazaar? A rummage sale? Bake sale? Thirty dollars."

"Just a meeting, Father, and we don't have thirty dollars."

"I'm sorry, Mrs. Gomez, but we're in debt for that hall, so we have to charge. And then there's cleaning, electricity, and so on. By the way, I haven't seen you in Church lately. In fact, I haven't seen you since I blessed your house last year."

"Thank you, Father."

Well, that was out.

"What did he mean, bless your house? If he did, it didn't work. Did you have to pay for it? Because if you did, maybe he could lend us the hall instead of refunding your money."

"It doesn't work that way, Tillie. Well, I guess we could try a school."

It seemed that the school also had to meet cleaning

staff prices, and, by a strange coincidence, it would also cost thirty dollars. Now what?

The Community Centre seemed a logical place to try, but on the other hand, we had already had some run-ins with the recreation department of the city over what activities we felt they should offer. They tended to favour candlemaking for housewives, drum majorettes for girls, and floor hockey for boys. There were also courses in making birds out of paper – I forget what the Hell those are called.

We tended to favour asking people what they wanted before planning; sometimes the most popular programmes were strange ones, sometimes they were practical. We had had a home barbering course at the same time as our self-defence one, and both had done pretty well. We had also had a dance for the under-twelve group, because that's what they wanted. I myself had been dubious about this one, since I think Barbie dolls and that kind of crap are already trying to make our kids grow up too fast. But my doubts were resolved at the first dance. They didn't dance together — they just exploded into a furor of activity more or less in time with the music, from three years of age up until about eleven; once they hit twelve they wanted to go to the older dance. At one point we even had a group called the Twelve Year Old Committee petitioning for the right to attend the teen dances. They lost.

The Community Centre, they were sorry to report, was booked for the next six months.

It looked like an impasse.

There must be a place a group of women could go and have a meeting we thought. Then it hit us! Of course! The Women's Centre!

We had never been there, but we knew where it was, and after all, we were women. So we caught a bus, and went to see them. We entered a slightly darkened room, where a group of women were sitting around on the

18

floor, listening in hushed silence to a record. It was a record about Emily Pankhurst. We waited politely until it finished.

"Wasn't that wonderful", breathed one of them, "how she reached out to the poor!"

Suddenly I didn't want to stay and be reached out to. One of our big headaches in organizing was that, whenever we managed to get a group together, some social worker or do-gooder would decide God or somebody had decided that they should come down and tell us what we wanted. We prefer bigots to do-gooders.

However, Chiclet was already talking. She explained what we wanted.

"A consciousness-raising session. But of course, you can join one of ours."

"We'd rather have our own," Chiclet stated firmly.

"But, Mrs. Gomez, we're all women together. Your problems are our problems . To be frank, the Centre is so busy, there isn't any night right now when it's not being used, but there is room in one of the sessions for you and your group. And we'd love to have you."

It was done. I was worried. Most people don't realize that poor people are the most conservative people in the world. That's because to us, experience has shown that any change is likely to be for the worse. This doesn't stop Chiclet and me from trying to organize against the Housing Authority, but it sure doesn't help. I figure the Authority was very smart when they picked that name. Most of our neighbours feel that any Authority is to be instantly Obeyed. Including husbands. This was one reason we wantad to have the session. We are also very conservative about sex. Contrary to popular opinion, most of us are still pretty puritan in our views on this. The sexual revolution is in about the same stage in our neighbourhoods as any other revolution. The talking stage. Of course, part of this is because a young girl from our income group doesn't have much to offer —

no diploma, no career, no family money, just herself. So she had better be damn sure the merchandise is all right. Chiclet and I don't agree with this opinion naturally, and we certainly don't believe that marriage to some schnook is a cure-all, but a surprising amount of our neighbours do, even if it didn't work for them.

So, when we arrived with our first group, I anticipated a little cultural shock. It started out quite well, in spite of the fact that the two groups had quite dissimilar views about what one wears to a meeting. Our people were mostly in dresses, having discarded their day-wear of jeans and dirty T-shirts, and sat on the chairs and couches. The Women's Centre group had discarded whatever they wear in the daytime for jeans and dirty T-shirts, and sat on the floor. I wore my pith helmet and sat on a cushion, and Chiclet paced around. The discussion began around the topic of husbands. That sounded fairly safe, and I cheered up. Our people weren't saying much, but they were listening.

"Well, when Neil and I got married, we agreed to each do our own thing. I wasn't going to give up my career, and he didn't have to give up his. Somehow, though, things haven't been the way I pictured them. He very rarely makes supper, and even when I remind him, he hardly ever remembers to put his dishes in the dishwasher. And he complains because I bring Stephanie to school in the morning, and he has to pick her up during rush hour. But he does agree that I need the car more than he does, because it's farther to where I work."

"It's very difficult for me to get across some of my ideas to Ben about how we could improve our relationship. He doesn't like the idea that I come down here and talk about our marriage in front of other people, although I'm sure he talks about it at the Squash Club."

Mrs. Grocholski stirred uncomfortably.

"Please participate, Sister."

"What do you do," she started out nervously, "if your husband hits you?"

"Yeah," said Georgia Wiseman, "and what if he starts yelling about clean floors right after he walks over them in his work boots?"

"If I had a husband like that, I'd leave," said one of the Centre ladies.

Linda Cunningham spoke up.

"I did," she said. "After my husband choked me, I left. I went to see a psychiatrist, and he told me everything would be fine if I would just do what my husband told me. Then I went to Welfare, and they didn't want to give me any money. They told me if I would just do what my husband said, maybe he'd come back."

"What was it you husband wanted you to do?"

"I think he wanted me to be someone else. He choked me because he couldn't find his clean socks. They were right where I told him."

Everybody started to talk at once, but they were not communicating. It was like the two groups of women were speaking different languages.

The chairperson called us to order. She said we would discuss wages for housewives. "I think everyone here would agree on wages for housewives, wouldn't we?"

One of the other women said "Well, if they're poor. But I don't see why some middle class woman should get paid to sit on her fanny while I go out and work."

"Wait a minute," said Linda. "You mean everybody who would rather stay home and raise her kids should have to crawl to her husband for money?"

"But what do you care? I said you should get it anyway."

"Where do you think we come from? Lower Slobbovia? I had a choice — poverty or a bad marriage, and I chose poverty."

There were some red faces, and some muttering, and our ladies got up to go, murmuring about baby sitters, and how late it was getting. Chiclet and I decided to stay. We thought it might be interesting.

"I'm sorry the other ladies had to go, Ms. Gomez. But I think you'll enjoy the next topic — "Can lesbianism be a political weapon?""

We never did find out.

Next week we're meeting with the Housing Authority. We don't like them, and they don't like us, but that's all right. We know where we are.

A REAL LADY

Chiclet and Linda and I were in Linda's house. I was standing on a chair in the kitchen searching the cupboards, Chiclet had a pile of coats from Linda's closet which she was busy going through the pockets of, and Linda was doing the same to a pile of jeans.

"A nickel! Here's five cents more."

"Good. How much does that make so far?"

"One ninety-five."

We had already ransacked Chiclet's house, and were finishing up on Linda's. Next we were heading for mine. It was the night before family allowance day, and we were all broke. We were also bored. We had decided to go down the street for a beer, but first we had to scrounge enough money for one each. It wasn't that we were thirsty, so much as we had decided to sample the local night life, and didn't feel we would be welcome unless we bought something.

I had great hopes of turning up something at my place, because I often forget to check the pockets of my coats. There is absolutely nothing so delightful as finding a treasure trove of a couple of dollars in a coat you haven't worn for six months. I have seriously considered planting money now and then, to make sure of a pleasant surprise from time to time, but then it wouldn't be a surprise. I also have a couple of places I've discovered over the years where I occasionally and absent-mindedly put change, but I wasn't as hopeful about them.

My place turned up a couple of large soft-drink bottles and a single dollar bill. We had enough.

The Beecham Hotel had been at its present location for about fifty years, and I had been at mine for ten, but I had never been inside. Linda had, once, but Chiclet was also a stranger. It was because of Linda's description of the place that we had decided to go. It sounded so awful we were fascinated.

We were all wearing coats, even though it was quite warm, because we wanted to be able to turn up our collars as we went in, so no one would recognize us. We slunk in, and it wouldn't have mattered anyway, because it was so dim in there that we could hardly see each other. We could also hardly breathe since it smelled as if at some time in the past the whole place had been awash in beer.

As we passed one table, somebody suddenly ducked, and I wondered who it could be. The only people we could think of who we might know in there were Mr. Grocholski, or possibly King Kong. That was one reason Chiclet had insisted on the coats, even though we thought that they would probably be on the men's side anyway. We had come in the door marked Ladies and Escorts. But neither of those two would have any reason to duck. Everybody in the project knew they spent quite a bit of time in there. I decided not to mention it, and to respect the privacy of whoever it was, in the hopes that they would respect mine.

Chiclet has accused me in the past of being a bit of a stuffed shirt, and I probably am. We hadn't even sat down yet, and I was uneasy. I wanted to go home, no matter how boring it was there, but I didn't want to be a spoilsport.

To my relief the table Chiclet selected was in a corner, and the only customer near us was a sweet-looking little old lady in a Victorian-looking dress. I decided she must be waiting for her husband. Sure enough, she was joined a few minutes later by an elderly gentleman. They seemed to be discussing something seriously. Suddenly her voice rose a little over the surrounding hum, and I heard her say "All right, you old barnacle, go home! I'll join these ladies at the next table." With that, she got up with great dignity and approached us. "Would you mind if I sat with you, dears? A lady isn't safe on her own in here. My name is Melicent."

Naturally, we said we would be delighted. Anybody could see she was a real lady. She had a little lace fichu at her neck, with a delicate cameo pin on it, and her snowy hair was drawn back in a bun. She had fragile-looking little hands, and her fingers were covered with rings.

"Is your husband joining us too?"

"My husband died in 1920, dear. Would you order for me? I must shake the dew from the lily."

She left a dollar on the table, and headed for the Ladies' Room.

The waiter arrived, and we ordered four beers. Melicent rejoined us, and began to talk about her early life, and about her father who was a minister. I began to relax a little, and took off my coat, thinking the rumours about this place must have been greatly exaggerated if a lady like this found nothing distasteful about it. Linda took out a cigarette. Melicent leaned over and placed her hand on Linda's.

"My dear, a lady doesn't smoke in public. Besides, you stay much younger if you don't smoke. How old do I look?"

"Uh, sixty?"

25

Melicent gave her little tinkling laugh. "My dear, that old fossil I was with was sixty. I'm ninety-two."

The waiter was back. "Is this old bat with you?"

Chiclet's tone was icy. "This lady is with us, yes. Why?"

"Because she's barred, is why. If I'd known she was with you you wouldn't have been served."

We all turned to look at Melicent. She laughed gently. "A misunderstanding, dears."

"Yeah?" said the waiter. "One more 'misunderstanding' and you never even get in the door again. And that goes for the rest of you broads, too."

I put my coat back on, humiliated. Barred from the Beecham Hotel! What a horrible threat! I wondered if they posted the names of people who were barred in some public place. If they did, I wasn't going to give my own name.

"Don't worry, dears. I've been thrown out of better places." Melicent didn't seem disturbed at all, but I did not find this observation comforting. She began to entertain us with stories about her dead husband, and her son who was lost at sea in 1918, and nothing else seemed about to happen, so I relaxed a little, and drank my beer. I was almost finished it, and thinking of leaving, when there was a sudden hush in the place. I looked up and the doorway seemed full of black-jacketed toughs.

"It's the Imps!" somebody whispered.

The Imps are the local motorcycle gang. I had thought the name was pretty funny, but I no longer felt amused. The leader had a pseudo-German helmet on, and a cigarette holder about nine inches long, and a beard. He didn't look too amusing, even though if I had heard the description I would have thought it sounded funny.

They swaggered through the room, and sat down two tables away. The leader took off his helmet, revealing two earrings in one ear, and none in the other. He also had tattoos all over his arms. I still didn't feel like laughing. He began ogling Linda openly. We were trapped. If we tried to leave, we would have to pass right by their table. Linda hunched down in her coat, but it didn't help. The leader summoned the waiter and pointed to our table. The waiter shook his head. The leader stood up and grabbed the waiter by his shirtfront. The waiter shook his head stubbornly and pointed to Melicent. The leader looked at her, shrugged, and jerked his thumb toward the door. We all stood up to go, except for Melicent. The leader came over and said "Won't all you ladies join us?"

Chiclet said "We have to go. The waiter won't serve us, anyway."

"Oh yes he will," said the leader softly. He sat down at our table, and the waiter hurried off. We were paralysed. The other gang members pulled their table over.

"Punks," said Melicent softly. Chiclet and Linda and I began to chatter loudly.

"No-goods," said Melicent a little louder.

The leader turned and looked at her. "You say something, lady?" he asked softly.

"Yes. I said you're a no-good bunch of hairy Neanderthals. I said you're so greasy you could baste a turkey by just waving at it. You need a good wash." She picked up her beer and dumped it on the leader.

He was so stunned he just sat there, but then somebody started to laugh. The whole gang stood up and surveyed the room.

"Something funny?" asked one of them dangerously.

"Yeah. You," said somebody at the other end of the room.

Chiclet jumped to her feet. "Time to shake the dew from the lily, dears." We all sprinted for the Ladies' Room, dragging a reluctant Melicent with us, and

27

locked ourselves in a cubicle.

After the noise of broken glass, screaming, shouting, cursing and police sirens had died down, we snuck out. There was nobody there but the waiter, sweeping up the debris. When he saw us he snarled.

"We're going," said Chiclet. "Don't worry, we won't be back. This place has no class."

"Yeah," said Melicent, "I've been thrown out of better."

We beat a hasty retreat.

The paper the next day said thirty people had been arrested in a tavern brawl, the cause of which had not yet been determined. They gave a list of names, but I didn't recognize any of them. I guess whoever it was who ducked when we went in gave a phony name. Good thing, too. There can't be a bigger disgrace than getting barred from the Beecham Hotel.

TEETH

How many people do you know who have no teeth? I mean, really none. Not even false ones. Every time I look around me, I see more and more people without teeth. It can really change your character.

Chiclet and I went together to have our teeth out. After five kids, I didn't have much left in the way of teeth anyway, but Chiclet's looked fine. It was her gums that had gone funny. Of course, we had both heard all about the Canada Food Rules, and how peanut butter is an excellent meat substitute. But hearing about them, and having them shoved down your throat, does no good if you don't have the money to follow them. So we compromised. We made sure the kids followed them. Somehow, we didn't think it was too important if we didn't get any milk or fruit.

We had a very funny month. I developed this allergy, or so I thought, and Chiclet started bleeding. Nose bleeds, mostly, but her teeth came loose too. You wouldn't believe it. We went to a doctor, and guess what? I had impetigo, and Chiclet had scurvy. Scurvy! I thought Captain Cook was the last person who ever had scurvy. It's like having beriberi. Right out of it.

I was humiliated about my impetigo. What was funny though, was that the night before, I had gone to a dance with Chiclet. I hadn't wanted to, because I was embarassed about my face, but Chiclet insisted. So I covered up my rash with Ozonol, and went. I was never so popular in all my life. Men kept asking me to dance and snuggling up to me. I finally decided Ozonol must be an aphrodisiac.

Anyway, our first reaction to having impetigo and scurvy was absolute horror. Our second reaction was to have something done. Chiclet went on massive doses of Vitamin C, but it was too late to save her teeth. Since I needed mine out anyway, we decided to go together, once my problem had cleared up. We booked two appointments with a dentist, and the rest of the time that we still had our teeth we spent gritting them so we wouldn't chicken out.

Chiclet's on Mothers' Allowance, so when she came out of the anaesthetic, they popped her new teeth right in. But I was working, and couldn't afford any new teeth. So I decided to gum it for a while.

After I had been home for a few days, Chiclet called. "Tillie guess what! We're going to be on television!"

"What?"

"Remember we wrote and asked the CBC to do a special on our recreation needs? Well, they called, and they want us to come on."

"You go."

"Not without you, Tillie. After all, you wrote the letter."

"I can't go. I can hardly talk, and I look awful."

Chiclet would not take no for an answer. I didn't know what to do. We had to have this programme so that we could embarass Recreation and Parks into doing something about the fact that we had no community centres in our areas, and no parks. But I didn't want

30

even my near and dear to see me without teeth, much less the entire city.

Did you ever notice how prevalent the letter "S" is? Almost every sentence uses either it or a soft "C". And I could not pronounce sibilants without any teeth. On the other hand, I have never won an argument with Chiclet. I didn't win this one either.

So, on a pleasant summer night, I found myself on the bus going to be interviewed on the Thee Bee Thee. In self-defence, I had done what I could. I was wearing my pith helmet, to give me confidence, and the shortest skirt I had ever seen. I figured if everyone was busy looking at my legs, they might not notice that I had no teeth. I was also muttering to myself. "Lethter Pearthon uthed to lithp. If it wath alright for Lethter Pearthon to lithp, it'th alright for me to lithp." I was also practicing keeping my mouth open with my lips closed. This was supposed to make people think I had something in my mouth, probably teeth.

When we got to the TV station, I almost panicked. I had forgotten all about makeup. We were ushered into the makeup room, and I tried to plot how to carry it off, while they made up Chiclet. I could be cool. "Teeth? How extraordinary. I'm sure I had some when I came in." I could refuse to wear makeup, and say I had a skin allergy. Now I regretted that my impetigo was cured. I could be noncommittal. "Teeth? No." I was still plotting when it was my turn. I sweated my way through getting my eyes made up, and my face powdered orange. Finally, they asked me to open my mouth. I closed my eyes. Nobody said a word. They acted like they had seen countless empty gums.

After that it seemed easy. All I had to do was watch my speech for stray "S"s and "C"s, and when in doubt cross my legs. This did result in some strange construction in my speech, however. I sounded very formal. Instead of saying "yes", I'd say "indeed", or "I

31

concur", or "agreed".

Watching the show later, I found that virtually all that was visible of me was helmet, glasses, and legs. I looked and sounded like a literate mushroom.

Strangely enough, we were successful, and we not only got the recreation department to come through, we got paid for the interview.

I used the money to make a down payment on some teeth. By the time I got them, I had learned to say "S" without teeth, and had to start all over again with a new lisp.

I've had no more problems with teeth.

Chiclet, on the other hand, keeps losing hers. They turn up in the oddest places. I've had to accompany her to bus terminals, schools, and restaurants in search of her wandering dentures. Strangely enough, they have never been found in any of these places. They always turn up safe and sound, somewhere at home. Once they were in her underwear drawer. During these searches, we have heard some very interesting stories about lost teeth from other sufferers. It seems to be a common problem. Teeth jump out in front of cars, make suicidal leaps down toilets and sewers, and hide under pillows. They also turn up in strange places on your person.

Chiclet just called. Her teeth are missing again, and her sink has backed up. I suspect a connection.

PRETTY PLUMBING

Chiclet and I were sitting at her kitchen table, drinking coffee and discussing the usual subject, Money, and How to Get Some. Maybe there are women somewhere whose usual subject is Men, and How to Get Some, but we don't know any. We're more likely to be plotting about how to get rid of them.

Over the years, we had considered various ways of getting our hands on some funds. Some of these were legal, some weren't. Somewhat reluctantly, we had always discarded the illegal ones. Not because they were illegal, necessarily, but because they were impractical. We aren't familiar enough with crime to really consider, say, robbing a bank.

At the moment, we were considering two courses of action. We could open a floating roulette parlour, or patent our new idea.

"I want to be a croupier. *Faites vos jeux, mesdames et messieurs, rien ne va plus.* Pretty classy, eh? I got that from an old radio programme!"

"Tillie, let's be practical. I think we've really got something with Bathroom Magic."

Well, she was probably right, but it didn't sound nearly as exciting as a gambling casino. But it would be a lot cheaper to start. We had already made a modest beginning.

It all started with Chiclet and I protesting the night school classes we got offered. We didn't even rate the cruddy ones other people got, like "Fun with Felt" or "How to Apply Makeup Properly". The ones they ususally tried to get us to take were "1,001 ways to Cook Hamburger" or "Are you Budgeting Wisely?" - courses we should have been teaching, not taking. Chiclet finally went over to the High School and began demanding plumbing, landscaping and car repair. We could really have used them. The school compromised and came out with a course called "Home Decorating on a Low Budget". I didn't go, because I figure if I can eat, sleep, cook and sit down in my house it's functional, but Chiclet went, because she gets bored with things the same way. She's always moving her kitchen around but it doesn't do any good. It still looks like everybody else's kitchen, because there's only two places to put the fridge and stove, and hardly any room for anything more. It's the same with the rest of the house. There just isn't room to be creative.

She came back from enrolling with a list of magazines she should buy. That was out, they were too expensive. We had to hit a lot of doctors' offices, because Readers' Digest and the National Geographic just wouldn't do. But we finally assembled a pretty good assortment, and off she went to night school.

I was still busy on my roulette idea. The more I thought of it, the better it seemed. How much would it cost to start, really? I began to assemble a list of items I would need. There was the wheel itself, of course. But that was easy. There was a miniature one at the corner store. I would need an eye shade, and a little rake, and some chips. Cards. Did you need cards for roulette? A

34

rule book, that was necessity. What else? Maybe I should think a little smaller. What would I need for a Floating Crap Game? I hadn't the faintest idea. But there must be some way to get in on the gambling craze that was holding half our tenants in the church hall to play bingo every week.

"Crap!" Chiclet came in like a late echo of my thinking. "Garbage! Nothing but ideas for making a charming playroom in your basement for only three hundred dollars. Tillie, we don't even have basements!" She threw her magazines on the floor.

"Well, let's not waste all that effort. Maybe there's something in here we can use." We began to look through the magazines. They were depressingly alike. To look at them, you'd think the entire world had enough money to give each individual in the family their own suite of rooms. Here was a chapter heading "A Charming Carousel for the 10 Year Old Girl". Here was her very own bathroom. The shower was surrounded by giraffes. What happened when she turned eleven?

"Tillie. Have you seen any bathrooms yet?"

"Have I! Every second page is on bathrooms."

"Did you notice anything?"

"Besides the fact that people have strange tastes, you mean?"

"Think, Tillie. what do we have that they don't?"

Son-of-a-gun! Not one of those bathrooms beautiful had a toilet! Here was an opening for our talents! All we had to do was to figure out a way to make the toilet an acceptable part of the décor, and we had it made. Conventional toilet covers obviously weren't doing the job. You know the ones I mean, those ratty little things in purple chenille that keep slipping off. We decided that what was needed was a whole new concept.

Total Bathroom Beauty - that became our watchword. We wanted to call our company Universal Can

35

Covers, but Chiclet thought that was too prosaic. We were going to be esthetic.

Obviously, we couldn't design the toilet in a vacuum, so we had to plan whole bathrooms. We began to think up themes.

"For Junior - we present a toy marching band. The centrepiece, charmingly disguised as a drum, is the toilet - heretofore a neglected and much maligned appliance. The bathtub is round, naturally, the soap is shaped like drumsticks, and the bathmat is a toy soldier!"

"Brilliant, Chiclet. But how do we disguise the toilet as a drum?"

We worked for days on this. Luckily, one of Chiclet's children had a doll's house with a toy toilet, and we wrestled with it and little blobs of material for some time. Finally, we had the basic design. No matter what the toilet was disguised as, it was a two-piecer. The part over the tank was one piece, and snapped on, and the part over the rest of it was made out of washable material, with elastic around the bottom, that just pulled off. It was sort of like a slipcover for a couch, but with a disguise built in with stiffening and cardboard. We began to manufacture miniature ones.

"How about the teenage girl? The toilet is disguised as a princess phone, the tank is an address book. Let's see, there could be shower curtains with phone numbers on them, and lipstick blots."

"For the husband — the toilet can be a golf ball!"

"Right. For the wife — a box of bath powder."

"For the bachelor — the rug can be a naked lady, and the toilet can be a bloodshot eyeball!"

"Chiclet — that's disgusting."

"Yeah, I know. Sure to be a big seller."

After we had ten or twelve little models, we began to worry about the next step. How to market our idea? We decided we didn't have the facilities to fill orders, so we should patent several designs, and sell the patterns to some of the magazines we had been looking at. Of course, neither of us knew whether the idea was patentable, so we decided to ask our alderman. He was a lawyer, and running for re-election, so we figured he'd be glad to give us some free advice.

On the morning he was due, Chiclet prepared her specialty, apple tarts with no apples in them, and I brought over some coffee. We had decided to be charming businesswomen for the occasion, so I regretfully left my pith helmet at home, and wore a suit. Chiclet wore shoes instead of sneakers, and took her hair out of its usual pigtails and put it in a bun. We looked terrible.

When the doorbell rang, instead of yelling "Come in, you're out!", Chiclet actually answered the door, and hung up the politician's coat. We graciously dispensed coffee and tarts before getting down to business.

At last, the psychological moment arrived. Chiclet whisked away his coffee cup, and replaced it with one of her models.

"Well, Bill," she said triumphantly, "what do you think of this?"

There was a long pause.

"Speaking of toilets," I said brightly, "we have an idea."

Two hours later, I left Chiclet's and went home to cook lunch for the kids. I didn't hear a thing they said. I was still puzzling over his last remark as he left.

"Listen kids, there's a lot of lonely businessmen in town, looking for a couple of bright girls like you. How about if I give them your phone numbers?"

"Are they interested in toilets, do you think?"

"Shut up Tillie," said Chiclet in a frozen voice. "Don't count on us in your next campaign, Mr. Friendly Politician. And don't slam the door on the way out."

All afternoon I spent trying to figure out what had

happened. One minute, we're all friends, the next ...Blooie! Suddenly, while I was washing the supper dishes, it hit me. We had been insulted!

I charged over to Chiclet's yelling "Chiclet! Chiclet! He insulted us!"

"Yes."

"What are we going to do?" I gasped. "Chiclet.. all the time he was here I thought he had a nervous twitch. Do you think he really meant to keep touching my knee?"

"Forget it, Tillie. He's strictly small potatoes. Our idea's still a good one."

"I don't know, Chiclet. Do you suppose the rug of the naked lady gave him the wrong idea?"

"That type is born with the wrong idea, Tillie."

"But he never did that before."

"You never took off your pith helmet or showed any leg before, either."

"Look, Chiclet, I've got a list made up of what we'd need for roulette. Let's go back to work on that one."

I didn't like how quiet Chiclet was. I was afraid she was going to challenge the alderman to a duel, or write a letter to the newspapers, or something.

"Listen Tillie. What about if it glowed in the dark?"

SNEAKER WEEK

"Tillie, what sounds better? Week of New Running Shoes, or Sneaker Week?"

"What are you doing?"

"I'm designing a new calendar. Sneaker Week, I guess."

I sighed. Chiclet was at it again. I could see she was well into whatever it was, because she was totally uninterested in the news that it looked like Father Florian was going to be purged. This was serious news. If they purged Father Florian, we would have to start all over with a new priest. Goodness knows it had been hard enough to work on Father Florian.

The Church is really a lot like the Housing Authority. Every time we went to work on a Board Member and convinced him that we were reasonable people with reasonable aims, his term ended, or he quit because his conscience couldn't stand it.

I had come over to consult with Chiclet on what to do about this latest piece of hard luck, and here she was designing a calendar.

"What's wrong with the calendars we have?"

39

"Come on, Tillie. The old ones are outdated. We know when all the holidays are; what we need is one that shows us which day the Family Allowance is coming, and when we should be planning big expenses. For instance, Sneaker Week starts on family allowance day in April. See? Then there's going to be School Clothes Week in August, Snow Wear Week in October, and so on."

"But what if people don't want to buy Snow Wear in October?"

"Tillie, do you always make pancakes on Pancake Tuesday? Of course not, but it helps you decide if you know when it is. This just gives you something to shoot for, and reminds you ahead of time what's coming up, so you don't spend the money on something else. For instance, if you know Sneaker Week is coming, you make sure you have income tax money left over for sneakers, see?"

"What else have you got?" I was beginning to get fascinated in spite of myself. It was true that calendars seemed sadly out of date. The only different calendars I had seen lately were the Women's Movement ones, with "Anniversary of Nellie McClung's speech to..." etc. Nice, but not too practical. Then there were the ones with fishing times on them, put out for men, and when the moon would be full. Maybe Chiclet had something.

"I was thinking of putting in a reminder right after the Christmas Holidays to start dieting for summer bathing suits. Maybe I could put Five Pound Week and Ten Pound Week, and so on. Then there's Buy Cough Medicine Now, and Think about a Garden Week in February when it's so depressing and everyone with money is in Florida."

We began to think about who would pay to have Chiclet's Calendar put out. Maybe we could get a running shoe company to pay for April, and Sneaker Week, and a seed catalogue company to pay for

40

February, and some diet food company to pay for January. I began to think furiously about what I always forgot was coming.

"How about Rubber Boot Week? Pajamas for Camp? Fund for Broken Windows? Haircut Day?

"How about January White Sales? I always forget them."

"I don't. I just never have any money left over. Chiclet, what are we going to do about Father Florian?"

"Are you sure about the purge?"

"Well, they offered him an extended stay at the seminary."

"It's a purge, all right.

Rats. When Father Florian first was posted to our parish, he was the model of a modern priest. I think he had a background in accounting. He wasn't fazed by the Pill, which Linda had sitting on her breadbox when he first came over, and was able to be quite rational on the subject of abortion. Chiclet and I have the same stand on abortion. We're neutral. Of course, this may be because neither of us is in danger of having any more kids. We've both had The Operation. But I figure you have to pass a test to drive, or to work in the government, or to go to university, but you don't have to pass a test to run for office, or to have kids.

Anyway, we had put a lot of work in on Father Florian. We had taken a young priest who knew nothing about the area he was working in, and shown him around, introduced him, and generally broken him in. He was just getting to the point where we had high hopes for him, and he was going to be recalled like a defective car. Obviously, our idea of a good parish priest, and the Church's idea were different. There was that unfortunate photo of him picketing the Housing Authority with us that turned up on the front page, and he had had a word dropped in his ear about letting us use the Church basement for a depot on the Great Garbage

March, although we took it all with us when we left. The last straw was probably the Family Life Education course in the church hall, which was really about birth control.

Still, he did all his regular work, too. He married people, and performed baptisms. For this he wore his uniform. I had gone to the baptism of Chiclet's last kid, and he had done a pretty good job. I was surprised that Chiclet had her kids baptized, but her idea of religion is pretty superstitious. She has a statue of St. Anthony that she stands on its head whenever she's lost anything.

"And you'll stay like that 'til I find it", she threatens. Strangely enough, her track record at finding lost objects is pretty good, unlike mine, but that may have something to do with personality. I'm sure I find a lot of things I've lost, but by the time I find them, I've forgotten they were ever lost.

Anyway, we've decided that we had better go higher up. Maybe we should talk to an Archbishop. After all, if we can get Father Florian's superiors to see that the Community values the work he does, maybe he won't have to be purged. So we're rounding up the regular church-goers among us. Chiclet doesn't go often, but at least she knows the routine, and the proper way to address an Archbishop, so she's organizing the visit. I'm not going, because somehow I don't think the word of a devout agnostic will count for much, and I don't know the right jargon. It took me a couple of years to understand what the bureaucrats in government were actually saying, and I'm not about to start deciphering the Church.

While Chiclet is talking to the Archbishop, I'm going to work on her calendar. I think there's a market for it out there, if we can just figure out who makes calendars. We may have it ready for 1980 - no that's a Leap Year - make it '81.

42

THE SWELL PARTY

Chiclet and I were very excited, but Chiclet wasn't showing it. Chiclet was being cool. I knew she was excited though, because she was actually thinking about what to wear. She couldn't go in jeans, because it was to be a swell party. We were being invited because we had worked to get the person elected who was throwing the party, and she had been. But it wasn't a campaign workers' party. We wore casual clothes to that one. This was a swell party, and I was bemoaning the fact that we had sold The Fur, and none of these people had ever seen it. One of us could have worn it one more time.

"Tillie, will you shut up for a minute about The Fur? I'm trying to figure something out."

It was the afternoon of the party, and we had scoured the neighbourhood for clothing. Everybody had contributed something, but the problem was how to make two outfits out of what we had. Two outfits, that is, where the dress bore some relationship to the shoes and the purse and the hair. I had been getting carried away. I had suddenly decided that pale green hair would carry anything I might want to wear, and probably highlight my eyes as well, but Chiclet had not been enthusiastic about the idea. Besides which, I had no idea how to metamorphose my hair into pale green. They don't seem to sell hair dye that colour. Then, too, Chiclet had merely said that I would look like I was wearing mashed peas, and I decided that wasn't the look I wanted.

The person we had got elected had promised, since she was also a single parent, that there would be plenty of men at the party. This added some agony to my apprehensions. The only men Chiclet and I had seen in months were busy driving buses, or taxis, or managing the Housing Authority, or voting at City Council, or something like that. I mean, they hadn't struck us as MEN.

So we really wanted to look nice, partly for our own reasons and partly to uphold the honour of public housing tenants. Georgia had been over, and offered us her new nail polish to paint our toes with, because to Georgia, that is the height of chic. Personally, I hate toes, dressed or naked, and I never leave mine nude if I can help it. I certainly don't draw attention to them.

Chiclet had abandoned the heap of clothes, and was looking speculatively at the curtains. I thought of the commercials for sheets where someone turns up wearing one, but my sheets were all flannelette, or mended.

Finally, Linda came in with a cape which added something to Chiclet's final choice, and I compromised with a dress I didn't really like that was mine anyway, but I added a necklace belonging to Mrs. Grocholski that gave it a certain air. I hoped.

By the time we left for the party, we were pretty giggly and nervous. Nobody would have recognized us. In fact, when we went to Linda's house so she could drive us, her oldest kid met us at the door with a polite, reserved-for-strangers-look that really made us feel different. Chiclet looked very exotic, and I prided myself that I didn't look too faded-housewife either.

When we got in the door, a little of my self-confidence started to ebb away, but Chiclet swept in, and met the occasion with all flags flying. As I attempted to follow her, I swept a little too hard, and the scatter rug I was standing on took off, and I sailed up to a little group of people with a fixed smile on my face and one foot furiously braking.

There was a small pause.

"Hello," I said brightly. "Why don't I go and take my coat off, and then I'll come back?"

I fled to the bedroom where Chiclet was removing her cape.

"Where were you?"

"Oh.. mingling."

Chiclet and I found the hostess in a circle near the middle of the room. She took us around to meet everybody.

"Now, girls," she said, "Jack and Bob are here, and they're in uniform, and I want you to leave them alone. They're mine."

One look at Jack and Bob, and we would have been delighted to leave them alone. Bob was extremely corpulent, and had a sash that encircled his uniform and stuck out in two funny little ends. Jack was extremely tall and thin, and his sash drooped down almost to his heels, and his moustache looked inclined to follow. Unfortunately, they both seemed fascinated by Chiclet so I abandoned her to her fate and went off to see what else was happening.

I found a group of people in the den, at least I suppose that's what it was. Anyway, it had a very African look, with zebra skins all over, a couple of leering masks, a drum in one corner, and the object of conversation being passed from hand to hand. It was a large stick with a knob which looked about as big as a grapefruit on one end.

A very good-looking male was explaining its function. "Magistrates in Africa carry them. You get to be a magistrate by fitting the knob in your mouth. This signifies that you won't use it to hurt anybody. Of course, nobody in this country has a mouth that big."

"Nonsense," I said brightly. By this time I had had two cups of very mild punch. It was sort of peach coloured, and was filled with fruit, so it couldn't possibly have been lethal. "I'm sure all races have basically the same mouth. See?" I opened my mouth. The knob wouldn't go in. I opened it wider. I passed the point of no return, and in went the knob. I shrugged gracefully. I yanked on the stick.

There's some snake somewhere whose teeth are slanted inward so that it helps him to swallow. You can never pull anything back from that snake though.

Walking around forever with a stick in my mouth wasn't what I had envisaged for the evening. People began to drift off in embarassed groups, and I was left alone with my problem. Once I was alone, there was a solution. I took out my teeth, and out came the knob.

I stayed for a while in the den, not really feeling like mingling, and then I decided I should look for Chiclet. Carefully avoiding scatter rugs, I made my way toward the source of the most noise. Sure enough, there she was. Part of the noise was from a disgruntled Bob. It seems he had sat on her to be playful and she was not amused. He was sitting on the floor, clutching her ankle.

"Oh, Tillie, there you are," she said coolly. "Is it time to go? I rather thought it was."

We had a tough time convincing Bob that he and Jack shouldn't drive us home, but our hostess came to the rescue, and reminded them that they had promised to stay and help clean up after the party, so we made our exit unescorted. I turned the wrong way off the step and stepped into a snowbank up to my armpits, but I think the door had closed by that time.

On the way home, we agreed that it had been an entertaining evening, but that we wouldn't want to do it too often.

I had a hard time trying to explain to Georgia how I had lost one of her eyelashes, because I really couldn't recall when I had had it last. Everyone agreed though, that it had sounded like a fun party, and they were a little wistful that they hadn't been there. We had to admit that Saturday night in the project looked dull by comparison.

THE LONG MARCH

Plod, plod, plod, shiver. Plod, plod, pluddle, plod, shiver. Plink, plink, plod, plod, shiver. It was raining, and we were going around in circles. Edna's curlers were trembling with suicidal raindrops which had not yet made up their minds to plunge. She was plodding in front of me, grimly holding her youngest by the hand, and muttering imprecations at the rain, the Housing Authority, and Chiclet. I was plodding behind Edna, who was plodding behind Linda, who was plodding behind Mrs. Grocholski, who was plodding behind me. In the middle was Chiclet, cheerfully giving directions.

"Close it up a little there, Linda. Hold your sign up higher, Tillie. People have to be able to read it. Edna, could you grab Tommie, he's going to kick Katie. Come on kids, why don't you sing something? How about 'Onward, Christian Soldiers'?"

Three of the younger children obediently started singing, but as they swung into Onward in various keys, my youngest started singing 'Rudolph the Red-Nosed Reindeer', being unfamiliar with hymns, and associating them all with Christmas. As this was

48

halfway through July, he was not only out of key but out of time as well.

My feet were wet. With every step I took, they slid halfway out the front of my sandals, and then my toes would hastily retreat from the cold puddles, and I would start to slip out the other end. I would have taken them off, and carried them, but in one hand I held a large sign, saying "Negotiate," and in the other I held my purse and a small hand.

Morosely, I wondered "What am I doing here? Why am I getting wet? Why am I getting a cramp in my arm holding a sign?" But I knew why. I was holding a sign, walking around in the rain, exposing myself and my child to pneumonia, because Chiclet had had an idea.

For months, we had been complaining to the Housing Authority that the rent was too high. It was alright for a while, but with inflation driving the cost of food upwards, and with Hydro going up, and Bell telephone escalating their rates, and clothing going up, and no change in income, it was getting very difficult to exist. The trouble is, we had run out of things to cut back on. If we cut back anywhere now, we would have no lights, or no phone, or no roof, or not enough food. So we decided that the institution we were most likely to be able to affect was the Housing Authority. Except we hadn't, yet. They explained that they could do nothing, it was up to the province. So Chiclet had written to friends in different parts of the province, and they were supposed to be outside of their Housing Authorities at that very minute, walking around in circles, and carrying signs. I had a deep-rooted suspicion that they were not walking around in the rain; either they were snug at home, or the sun was shining where they were . I really couldn't see another group of people being this dumb. I was about ready to quit, and squish on home, when the Press arrived. I perked up a little, and tried to straighten out my soggy sign, and wipe my kid's nose,

49

and generally be a credit to Chiclet.

"Ms. Gomez?"

"Here," she waved.

We parted to let the press through, and closed ranks again. This was Chiclet's idea. She figured if she was interviewed inside the circle, it would look as if there was an endless line of marchers behind her, as we went round and round. We turned our signs so they would be picked up by the cameras. They said, all together, "Negotiate Lower Rents Now Please." Edna was carrying "Please," which was probably a mistake, since her face did not look as if that was what she meant. But none of us looked particularly cheerful, except Chiclet.

Linda's hair was hanging in wet strings, and occasionally whipping back to lash Edna in the nose. Mrs. Grocholski looked like a dispirited currant bun, but I had my pith helmet to keep the rain off my glasses, for which I should have been grateful. The children were being kept from whining with promises of visit to a real restaurant, with hot chocolate. Out of the corner of my eye, I could see Georgia Wiseman, whose big contribution had been to get us a drive to the Housing Authority. She had refused to picket, because she didn't want to get her new hair-do wet. She was sitting in her husband's car, pretending she didn't know us.

The press left. Chiclet said "All right, we can go to the restaurant now."

The kids were starting to cheer as Edna said "Wait, Chiclet. As long as I'm here, I might as well pay my rent."

"Oh, good. Wait a minute. Tillie, Chiclet, I want to pay mine too."

Linda headed into the building with Edna, and after a minute, the rest of us followed. All of us vaguely felt that they might need some support. As we piled into the elevator, a man joined us, and took stock of our signs, the children and the damp without betraying any

50

expression at all. We left the signs in the elevator.

As we got to the counter to pay the rent, the girl behind the desk said "Is that crowd still out there picketing?"

We tried to look innocent, and the man from the elevator spoke up. "Sure are," he said, "Must be about thirty of them by now."

I edged over to the window. Nobody out there.

"Really!" said the girl. "Mr. Prentiss! This man says there are thirty pickets out there now."

Mr. Prentiss was heard to remark that somebody had better do something.

After paying the rent, and treating ourselves and the kids to hot chocolate, we piled into Georgia's car.

"Georgia, you didn't see anybody else picketing, did you?"

"In the rain? Of course not."

That night, we saw ourselves on television, solemnly going around and around. The announcer said that a reliable report put our numbers at around thirty, and that tenants in other centres had been marching, too, with equally large turnouts.

Mr. Grocholski just got home from work in time to see Mrs. Grocholski and his kids on a picket line, and hit the roof. He's forbidden her to have anything to do with me and Chiclet, and our crowd.

Every time we hear the story of our picket, the numbers grow. Chiclet and I figure if we could just get our money to work like that, we'd have it made.

The province has said that they will consider lowering the rent, for what that's worth, and I've got a dandy cold, and a huge blister on one foot.

INSPECTIONS

Chiclet's kitchen looked rather like something out of a war film about refugees. Distraught women were milling around, clutching parcels and animals of varying descriptions, and there was a steady hum of noise. In the middle, calm and collected, was Chiclet.

"What's going on?"

Immediately, a babble broke out, with five or six people talking at once.

Chiclet raised her voice a little. "Where have you been, Tillie? It's inspection time again."

"Not again! I just got over last year's trauma." Ordinarily, I don't believe in waxing floors. So I don't. I never have to worry about stripping my floors. They get waxed once a year, before the inspection. I hate the inspection. I hate feeling helpless and frustrated as the Housing Authority marches through my house, making judgements. Of course, one of the reasons that I hate being judged by my housekeeping is that it's terrible. I never know where to put anything, and, as a result, my house is always cluttered.

Chiclet, on the other hand, seems to keep house effortlessly. I never see her running around cleaning, but it just seems to stay clean. She never worries about inspections. She lets them in, tells them what she wants fixed, and that's that. That's why everybody was over at Chiclet's. I finally realized that the object that Edna was holding was a giant turtle.

"Will you take Chicken, Chiclet?"

"I hate to break this to you, Edna, but that's a turtle."

"I know, Tillie, but my youngest has never seen a chicken, except cut up and cooked, and he insists that this is a chicken. So that's his name."

"Why are you hiding him?"

"Because we're only supposed to have one pet. We have two."

"Why don't you put him in a dresser drawer? They're not supposed to look in there. And you'd sure find out if they do or not." We began to laugh at the thought of dicovering Chicken lurking in piles of underwear, but Edna was not amused. Chiclet agreed to harbour Chicken in her laundry sink, and Edna left, relieved.

"I've got to run, Chiclet. It's going to take me all day to make a dent in my house. When are they coming? Tomorrow?" The Housing Authority has to give twenty-four hours notice, in writing, but quite often it's a loose impression of twenty-four hours, and works out to something like eighteen. You get the notice at four in the afternoon, and they're due at ten in the morning. Last year I was up most of the night, waxing and singing Christmas carols. I always sing Christmas carols when I wax. Whatever reason there is for this is well hidden in my subconscious, and I'd just as soon it stayed there.

"Wait a minute, Tillie. I'll go with you, and give you a hand. What about you, Linda? Want to come over to Tillie's, and we'll help her find places to put things?"

Chiclet rounded up a squad. Linda, Mrs. Grocholski, and Chiclet all accompanied me back to my house, carrying mops, and pails, whatever brand of wax everyone was now swearing by, and polisher. Once we got there, I didn't know where to start. That's the main problem with my housekeeping. I don't know what activity logically follows another. I get so fouled up trying to work out a system, nothing ever gets done.

"Tillie, you start in your bedroom. Shove everything into your dresser drawers. We'll worry about anything that doesn't fit later. Linda, you take the other bedrooms and the bathroom. Mrs. Grocholski, you take the living room. I'll take the kitchen and the laundry room."

Chiclet had, of course, taken the hardest job. Everything I didn't know what else to do with was in the laundry room. Luckily, Chiclet knew enough not to ask me where to put something. Somehow, she always found a place. She started to work with a will, so I trudged upstairs to my bedroom.

Where did everything come from. Oh Lord, here was that insane nightgown I bought by mistake at the rummage sale. What on earth was I going to do with it? On top of my dresser was the odd sock basket. There must be something I could do with all those odd socks. Maybe I could make stuffed toys. Socks make great hand puppets. You just slip them on your hand, and double the toe back, and you've got a mouth. It looks like a worm. If I just add two buttons for eyes, and a big red button, that's perfect for a nose. Let's see. Where's that old stuff the Easter eggs came in, that I was saving for something like this? It would make perfect hair.

"Tillie, what are you doing?"

"Oh. Oh, hi. I'm trying to figure out what to do with all these socks. Isn't this a nice worm family? And I've been writing a script....."

"It's lovely Tillie. But why don't you just throw out the socks?"

"Throw them away? But what if the other ones turn up?"

54

"Then you throw them away too. By the way, I just threw out thirty-five egg cartons that were on top of your refrigerator. Were you saving them for something special?"

"No. But I kept thinking that there must be something I could do with them. All those columns in the paper tell you what to do with old things you have lying around, and I'm sure there's going to be a column on egg cartons pretty soon."

"Well, that's too bad. Linda said she threw out a whole bunch of toilet paper and paper towel rolls. What were you going to do with them?

"Oh, I was going to make puppets out of them. You use the toilet paper rolls for arms, and the paper towel rolls for legs, and you attach strings to them, and then..."

"Never mind, Tillie. After the inspection, you can start saving again. But you know you never get around to actually doing anything with them. Why don't you go downstairs, and I'll finish up in here?"

"Okay. I was thinking about making a pillow slip out of that awful nightie. What do you think?"

Chiclet showed me gently out the door, and closed it firmly. I wandered downstairs. It looked like somebody else's house. I hardly recognized it. It was so bare.

"Where is everything?"

Linda asked "Do you like it, Tillie?"

"Yes. But where is everything?"

"Well, Chiclet said to throw most of it out. Don't look, Tillie. If you don't know what went, you won't miss it."

By the time the inspection team came the next morning I was ready, thanks to the mop patrol. I was fairly calm even. I was a little nervous because I had the uneasy feeling that possessions might come exploding out of cupboard doors, or falling off shelves at any moment. Even with six garbage bags discreetly hidden

55

in the garbage house, I felt in my bones that there was an avalanche waiting for someone.

The Housing Authority was very pleased with the condition of my floors and walls. I decided not to tell them that it was due to my firm policy of never waxing floors, and rarely washing walls. Most of my neighbours who were better housekeepers had washed all the paint off their walls, but mine still had the original paint in good shape. They couldn't figure out how mine was still fine, but the obvious conclusion didn't come to them.

It's times like these that I would give anything for a basement where I could store things. Until they left, I was very jumpy, running interference, in case anything looked like it had a suspicious bulge; but things stayed in place, and I actually got a look of approval from them.

Of course, the next day, the paper featured a column about what to do with old egg cartons. I clipped it out and it's here someplace, along with the one on old bleach containers.

I knew vaguely that there was something missing, and this morning I discovered what it was. There in the freezer was my ironing. I hate ironing, so I think I'll leave it there for a while. Anyway, the cold is good for it, Chiclet says, and makes it easier to iron. And Chiclet is the one who should know.

I wonder if tablecloths can get freezer burn?

GREEN THUMBS

Last year Chiclet and I tried our hand at gardening and we actually grew some vegetables, so this year we're mounting a campaign to get garden plots for public housing tenants.

As a first step, Chiclet wrote a letter in April asking the government for some plots. She was told there weren't any; they were all allotted. She got quite annoyed and together we wrote a blistering letter. We got a reply saying we could have three plots.

Success! But there are a few drawbacks. None of us have cars. We can take the bus to the plots, but we aren't sure that we'll be allowed on the bus with rakes, and hoes, and shovels. But we're still pretty enthused about it. And we're determined not to make the mistakes we made last year.

Last year, we dug up our back lawns to make gardens. Chiclet planted pumpkins, and then detailed the kids most likely to pull them up to stand guard, promising them each a pumpkin at Hallowe'en if they did a good job.

I planted the usual: tomatoes, and cucumbers, and radishes, and lettuce, and green onions, and green peppers, and carrots, and peas, and then I threw caution to the winds, and planted kohlrabi. This was because as a child I had tasted it once and loved it. But supermarkets never seem to carry it and I hadn't tried it since. So when my kids asked what it looked like, I was pretty vague. We didn't do so much weeding last year because I didn't know what was supposed to be there and what wasn't. I had planted so much stuff, on so little ground that I just let everything except dandelions alone.

We had a very good salad early in the year, mostly weeds. I threw in lamb's quarters that were growing wild, and what looked like shamrocks, but tasted salty, and some nasturtium leaves from the front garden and some chives, and a few radishes. It was delicious. But that seemed to be the high point. I couldn't identify much of what was growing, except for the tomatoes and cucumbers. It started to look like a jungle out there and the neighbour's cats began turning up to prowl through the foliage and lurk in hiding to pounce on any poor unsuspecting twirp of a dog that wandered by. I began to worry about going out there myself, and would dart in and grab something that looked edible. My kids loved it. They could lie in it concealed and nibble. My youngest kept pulling up the carrots to see what was happening, but nothing was.

One day one of them came in with a queer-looking thing and asked what it was. My first reaction was horror. They had started to mutate out there! Then I thought there might be some horrible parasite lurking in there along with everything else. Finally, it occurred to me that it might be a kohlrabi. It was. Somehow they had never told us about this vegetable in school. I had seen root vegetables, and stalk vegetables, and vegetables that are actually the fruit of the plant, like peas and cucumbers, but never had I ever seen a vegetable before that couldn't make up its mind. This bulge develops halfway up the stem and starts to put out leaves, and that's a kohlrabi. It looks terrible but the few I got were good.

But while I was harvesting my kohlrabi, and looking in vain for my green peppers, and trying to salvage enough peas from my greedy children to make one meal of, the tomatoes were being active behind my back. Soon I had baskets and baskets of tomatoes, and they still kept coming. In desperation, I decided to make tomato soup. I had seen a friend make it years before, and I remembered that she said you had to put in baking soda, to cut the acidity, before you added milk. I had so many tomatoes, I decided I would need a cup of baking soda.

I wish I could forget what happened. The kitchen and I were immediately covered in pink foam. It oozed over the stove and floated to the windows, clung to the screens, and swam underfoot.

Chiclet came in, and as it attached itself to her, she turned a little pale, and asked what it was. Her relief was enormous when I told her. She thought it looked as if someone had exploded. I thought it looked like some special effects for a space movie where someone's face mask comes off. It was macabre.

Anyway, we just turned off the stove and left. When I ventured back, after fortifying myself at Chiclet's with some coffee, most of it had dried. It didn't improve the looks that much, but it was easier to handle.

Occasionally, I still find little bits of it hiding and trying to breed in corners, but it's losing.

So this year, only one of us is going to plant tomatoes. And it isn't going to be me. I'm going to learn from last year, and plant peas and cucumbers. Chiclet is off pumpkins, because after all her work she only got enough to pay off her corps of guards. She's going to plant corn and carrots and green peppers. Linda is planting tomatoes and onions, and Edna is planting cabbages and lettuce. Mrs. Grocholski is planting eggplant and squash.

I don't know how we're going to get all this stuff home at harvest time, or what I'm going to do with my share of the eggplant, but I'll worry about that in the fall.

FOOT-IN-MOUTH

Chiclet and Linda both suffer, to some extent, from a disease we call Foot-in-Mouth. The cause seems to be an inability to wait until the brain is functioning before opening the mouth. Conditions which seem to bring on this disease are usually the close proximity of a male with whom one has had a former relationship, or the proximity of a male with an unfortunate opinion of females.

Because this seems to be a little-recognized disease, we thought we might print up a booklet to warn women of typical signs which might herald the onset of an attack, as well as some of the better-known symptoms.

The classic symptom is, of course, the utterance of the following phrase: "Go ahead and hit me, then, if it makes you feel more like a man." Another is the famous sarcastic laugh, following the reply to the question "And where have you been until this hour of the morning?" (This question is one of the signs of a possible attack.) More well-known are the stigmata which appear on the body after the onset of the attack:

the well-known black eye, broken jaw or sprained ankle.

This disease is practically confined to women, although some teen-agers of both sexes, and the occasional younger child do show early symptoms. These symptoms are usually of the "Try and make me" or "You and whose army?" variety.

Some sufferers have chronic Foot-in-Mouth, while others have only occasional attacks. Those suffering from the occasional attack can sometimes trace the triggering influence to an unaccustomed intake of alcohol.

"Linda, you're the one who has the most experience with this problem. What would you say was the underlying cause?"

"Stupidity."

"Oh, come on, Linda. You're not stupid. There has to be something else."

"Well, I guess you could call it the 'Too-late-smarts.' Most people's brains say 'No, I shouldn't say that.' Mine says 'Woops, I shouldn't have said that.'"

Chiclet said "I think we should include some typical case-histories, too. What about the time what's-his-name was throttling you out in the back yard? How did that start?

"I think it started when I said 'Supper's over. You missed it.' Then we had the usual squabble. Then he put his hand on my throat, and I said 'Why don't you strangle me out in the back yard, in front of the neighbours?' So he did. The signs following this attack were purple stripes on the throat, grass stains on the rear, and the arrival of the police."

"I remember that one. He turned up at my door the next day, with several threats to pass on to you."

"That's right, Tillie. And then he said he didn't hold it against you."

I should say right here that there was absolutely no reason why he should have. I didn't keep him late for

62

supper, and I wasn't even there. But for some reason, I seem to get a certain amount of the blame for the onset of these attacks. Chiclet also is blamed for some of them. There may be a small amount of justification in this, as Chiclet does have a habit of saying things like 'The so-and-so. And you believed him?' Or 'Don't put up with it any more. Throw the bum out!' However, these are really only sympathetic utterances, not deliberate attempts to incite to riot. She's really just being a polite audience, booing and hissing when the villain makes an entrance, and cheering the heroine on.

I was puzzled too that I was held to blame for some of this, because my separation had been almost painless. My husband had just started coming home later and later, and leaving earlier and earlier, so that when he left, I didn't know it for about a week. Then it gradually seeped in. I think what really brought it home was the absence of laundry. No more embarassing incidences of underwear that mysteriously turned pink in the washer. No more grilling about why he always got back less socks than he put in. No more having to conceal a favorite garment which had suddenly shrunk.

Since then, I have always shied away from any relationship with a particular man, since it always seems to get right back to socks and underwear. Oh, it starts off innocently enough.

"Honey, I seem to have popped a button. Could you sew it back on?" But I know what that means. One step more, and his laundry turns up.

Most of the time, I could trace no possible connection between any action I had taken, and the resulting blame. When I was in the hospital with a broken foot, Georgia had phoned me and said "Tillie, this is Georgia. I just phoned to let you know I'm not allowed to talk to you anymore." I never did find out what I'd done that time. By the time Georgia was allowed to talk to me again, she didn't want to discuss it.

Sitting there with Linda and Chiclet discussing past history really made it come alive again. Of course, there were occasions where someone got thumped without ever having opened their mouths. Mrs. Grocholski almost never says 'Boo' to Mr. Grocholski as far as we know, but he thumps her out pretty regularly. I guess it probably has to do with the fact that his paycheck doesn't grow any bigger, and he's at the age when he knows it isn't going to, and she's the handiest person to thump.

But even when Foot-in-Mouth has struck, so what? What price freedom of speech? We forgot all about the fact that we were supposed to be writing a book on preventive medicine, and began to discuss how to strike a blow for women.

The upshot was the formation of a musical group called the Freedom Trio, which, accompanying itself on combs and tissue paper, did a buck and wing into Linda's house through the back door and down the hall, stopping only long enough to thumb its noses in unison at the presence on the couch, and out the front door and back to my place.

Linda's not allowed to speak to me any more. I don't know how come it's all my fault, unless it's because I'm the only one who knew the dance steps.

THE BIG TIME

"Politics –
A game for hicks
And dried-up sticks
Is politics."

If that sounds like sour grapes, it was. The grapes were about as sour as they could get. I plunked my ukeline petulantly. It sounded terrible. This was only partly due to the fact that I don't know how to play the thing.

"Tillie, will you knock it off? Just stop singing and stop plunking. Things are bad enough without that too."

Bad? Things were terrible. We had just lost the election. By a landslide. It was a hot, sultry night in the project, and everything smelled of Noxema. We sat on my back steps, sunburnt from campaigning, and generally dejected. Even my pith helmet hadn't prevented my getting a severe noseburn, and obviously the midges loved Noxema. They kept landing on my nose and getting their feet stuck.

"What went wrong?"

"I guess they're just not ready for us yet, Tillie."

"But Chiclet, even our own people didn't vote for you." We were pretty certain of this, because out of the whole city, Chiclet had received forty votes in her campaign for mayor. There were more than forty families in our project alone, to say nothing of the other twenty-five or so projects in the city. We had figured that with all the poor people in the public housing projects behind us, we had a pretty good chance. But it hadn't worked out that way at all.

"Maybe King Kong was right. He said if I was running I should get my hair done and wear a dress. And no sneakers."

"Chiclet, when was your ex-husband ever right? That wouldn't have been you. You probably would have lost the other thirty-eight votes."

"I don't know, Tillie. Maybe this time he was right. I guess nobody wants a mayor in pigtails and blue jeans."

"Maybe you should have changed your sex while you were at it." This did not get a rise out of Chiclet. I was worried. She'd lost all her bounce. We hadn't really thought she'd win. . . well, once in a while, maybe, we'd get carried away, and talk about it as if she could, but deep down we'd known better. The city had never had a poor mayor, and there was no sign that they had suddenly decided it was time for one. Women hadn't exactly been popular politically either. So we hadn't really thought that a single parent mother named Chiclet Gomez, who lived in public housing and was supported by the City, would be the people's choice. We did think, though, that the other single parent mothers in the project would vote for her. After all, when anything went wrong, who did they call? Chiclet. If they didn't get their cheque, they called her. If Welfare insulted them, they called her. If the Housing Authority hassled them, they called her. If the School Board gave their kids a hard time, they called her. So why didn't

66

they vote for her? That's what really hurt.

"You should run for office, Chiclet," they'd say, "then we'd get some attention paid to us."

To tell the truth, we didn't exactly suffer from lack of attention, so much as the wrong kind of attention. If the crime rate in the city went up, the papers would write deep stories about how we breed crime in the projects. Taxi drivers would direct strangers in town to our neighbourhoods, where they would wander up and down looking for red lights. City politicians would loudly bewail the amount of "taxpayers' dollars" being spent on us. Cops would assume that a baseball team was actually in all probability a gang of purse-snatchers out to mug some little old lady. We were fed up.

Chiclet had written to the editor of a local newspaper offering to visit any project in the city at midnight with him. She told him it was safer than the better-off neighbourhoods, because we didn't have anything anybody wanted. He never answered. He didn't publish the letter, either.

The truth is, we're proud of where we live. We have neighbours. "Well, everybody has neighbours," you might answer. That's not true. Oh, it's true that everybody has somebody living near them, but we have *neighbours*.

Take the time that Linda Cunningham's little boy had a broken leg. By the time she got outside to him, somebody had called an ambulance; somebody else was holding his hand, saying what a brave boy he was; somebody else was holding his glasses; Georgia Wiseman said she'd go to the hospital with Linda; and Mrs. Pettigrew offered to do her dishes and mind her other kids till she got back. When Linda came back about midnight, Chiclet and I went over to see if there was anything we could do. I was putting on the kettle to make her some tea when the doorbell rang.

"I'll get it, Linda. You just sit down and have some of

that tea Tillie's making."

It was the police. They'd got an accident report. They came barrelling in like we'd committed a crime. It was a good thing Chiclet was there. They started making cracks about the neighbourhood, and implied that either this seven-year-old hood had got caught in a rumble, or that this seven-year-old angel had been beaten by a vicious child-beater, namely his mother. Poor Linda. She was worried, and exhausted, and this was the last straw. She started crying and sort of hiccupping. I put my arms around her and I started crying too. Chiclet told them to get out. Then she phoned the station and told them off. Then we put Linda to bed. Chiclet was so mad she sizzled.

It was so typical.

"Some kid falls off a swing somewhere else, everybody says that's too bad. Here it's not possible. Somebody had to be doing something bad. How come?"

Well of course we knew the answer. Let the City realize that we are just the same as everybody else, except that we have no money, and they'll have to examine the way they treat us. But as long as they can tell themselves that we're poor because we deserve to be, then they don't have to worry about how they treat us, short of outright extermination. Actually, a couple of rednecks had proposed that we all be sterilized, but it had never got to a vote.

But you can see why Chiclet ran for mayor. It was turning into Them against Us, and Us was mainly composed of women, children, old people and cripples. Of course, that's not who the forces of Them claimed they were fighting. There were long speeches about cheaters on the welfare system, and how the truly needy suffered. The only family I knew that was ripping off the system, with both a job and welfare, was still not making enough to move out of public housing. We had discovered that ripping off the system is only unforgiveable if you don't do a good job of it. After all, there are companies making millions of dollars whose sole purpose in existence is to show people how to rip off the system at income tax time. Of course, it only works for you if you have money.

So Chiclet decided to expose the whole rotten system by running for mayor. We had considered becoming revolutionaries, but not very seriously, in spite of the fact that every summer a horde of young social workers with Marxist leanings would get so depressed and infuriated by the system that they would come into the projects yelling "Man the Barricades!" "Revolt!" You can get hurt that way.

I used to worry about our Hungarian neighbour, Mrs. Szabo. She was a refugee, and I wondered what her reaction would be to Communists on her doorstep. It wasn't what I thought it would be.

"I feel I should tell them, Tillie, but the young - they don't listen. We had a lot of fine young people like that in Hungary, idealists, you know, before the Communists came in. When things got bad, they stood up and said 'Hey! That's not what you told us!' They were the first ones shot."

So Chiclet and I decided that our way would be strictly constitutional. We'd go to the people. So we did. And the people had rejected us.

The question still remained: why? We sat there, too dejected to move from the stoop, even when it began to rain. After all, why shouldn't it rain on us? Everything else had happened. Not only had we lost the election, we were now in the hole financially. Again. It wasn't that we mounted an expensive campaign. Far from it. We had mainly relied on the fact that if one candidate got coverage, everbody running for that office got coverage. Besides that, we had rallies in the projects, and they had gone well. But still, there were unavoidable expenses.

We had to have a couple of posters, and there were coffee parties, and transportation for our candidate from one end of the city to the other.. well, anyway we were in the hole. Not by much to any of the other candidates for mayor, but two hundred dollars to us was equal to about ten times that much to the others. After all, neither of us worked, where were we to get two hundred dollars?

"Chiclet," I finally said, "why don't we go and get bombed at somebody else's victory party? There'll be music, and free booze, and not too many speeches, and we won't have to sit here in the rain."

"Tillie, I feel rotten. I'm damned if I'm going to go and look like a good sport. I'm not a good sport. I'm mad. But you don't have to sit here in the rain just because I am. You go if you want to."

Well, naturally I wasn't going to go alone. After all, I was Chiclet's campaign manager. So we sat there.

Suddenly, somebody cleared their throat. Linda Cunningham materialized at our side.

"Chiclet," she said hesitantly, "could you come to my place a minute? I need to talk to you."

I could see Chiclet wanted to be left alone to mope, but what could she do? She always came if anybody needed her. So we got up and went over to Linda's. As we stood there in her hallway, wringing out our hair, I could hear vague muffled squeaks from the living room. Mice? Suddenly, all the lights came on. "Surprise! Welcome to the victory party!"

"But I didn't win!"

"I know, Chiclet...but, well, we did." It was Edna speaking. In spite of the party, she was still wearing her curlers, but she was all dressed up. "You're going to be mad, Chiclet, but we thought a lot about it, and we didn't want you to win. We thought, if you won, and you were the mayor, you'd forget about us. After all, you'd be making a lot of money, and you'd have

70

to move out, and everybody would want you to listen to them, and...well, we want you here."

"You nuts! How could I forget? This is family! Give me a beer, somebody!"

It was okay. It wasn't that nobody loved her. It was the opposite.

It was a great party. After the booze was all gone, we went to the Mayor's victory party. While Chiclet went over and buttonholed the Mayor, and told him exactly what our people wanted and expected this term, the rest of us discovered a fountain of free booze. It was mixed with orange juice.

The next morning, I was ready to bid goodbye forever to political life. I couldn't look my orange juice in the eye, and I couldn't quite remember what I'd said to the Mayor's aide, but I could remember the look on his face quite clearly, so I had the feeling it was probably not polite.

Since then, though, Chiclet and I have been thinking. At least they know we're here, now, and every so often the papers call us to see what we think about something. It's not too soon to begin planning for the next election. We've paid off our debt and we've been working things out...see, if I ran for mayor the next time, they wouldn't worry about losing Chiclet, and I wouldn't have to move if I put half the salary into a community office, and some of the people around here could get a job, and...everything would look really good if Chiclet would just stop looking at the Prime Minister that way. Like she might have a better idea.

THE MAD SNICKERER

You may find this hard to believe, but Chiclet Gomez is as well known in her milieu as, say, Elizabeth Taylor is in hers. But not for the same reasons.

City Hall officials know Chiclet. As a matter of fact, the one big similarity between them and our neighbours is the way both react to the sight of Chiclet bearing down on them. They panic. I must admit that, even though I am Chiclet's best friend, there are times when I have the same reaction. Somehow, whenever I listen to Chiclet, I have the feeling I'm going to end up in trouble.

When Chiclet and I organized the Self-Defence for Women course, it looked fairly straightforward. Chiclet was reading an article on rape, and it had some pretty frightening statistics in it. It said that something like one in every ten women is attacked, and, like Chiclet pointed out, we were long overdue. A hundred and ten women live in our project, not to mention teenage girls, and not one of us had been attacked in the past ten years. So we decided we'd better get ready.

Actually, I have my own theories about this. If I'm out late at night, I clench my fists, hunch up my shoulders, and stomp like I'm wearing army boots. So far, this works fine. Another of my theories is that none of the males who live in our community would dare mess around with me or Chiclet, and nobody else would dare to be caught in here at night. Robbers and kidnappers don't consider public housing an ideal site for business either, so that only leaves the insane axe-murderer. He's the one I worry about.

I don't really know why Chiclet would worry. Not that I'm implying she's not attractive, but she could lick a cageful of bears without thinking twice.

Look at the time we had a riot at the community centre dance. There we were, two ladies selling tickets, the place was crammed with teenagers, all laughing, dancing, necking, and generally behaving themselves, when suddenly a teenybopper with a bass voice came pounding down the basement stairs. "They're here!" he yelled. Instantly, mass evacuation. Even the musicians left. Chiclet and I were just beginning to ask 'Who?' when they all poured back in.

"They're not here."

"Naw, they're probably not even coming."

"Who's not here?" we asked. We were met with bland, polite, inquiring looks. The musicians picked up their instruments.

"They're here! This time they're really here!"

This time we left too. It was a rumble. What a sight! Weapons were appearing like magic. A boy with legs about four feet long pulled a six-foot long pair of gardening shears out of his pants. Had he been *dancing* like that? Baseball bats, fish knives, a shovel, brass knuckles (I thought they were just in books!), billy clubs, chains, you name it – they had it. And that was just our side.

Chiclet was furious. How dare they wreck our dance!

She was in and out like a hornet. "Give me that! Hand it over! I'm ashamed of you. What were you going to do with that? Get back in the hall we paid good money for. You get back in there and enjoy yourselves if you know what's good for you."

She went up to the leader of the other side. He was wearing an ascot. She flicked it contemptuously. "Look at you! You call that dressed for a rumble? Someone could strangle you just by pulling your tie. You kids today don't know anything. Go home!"

By the time the police arrived, Chiclet and I had dropped the weapons in a nearby fountain, there was a peaceful dance going on, and the visitors had departed. It was the first and last rumble we ever had.

So I couldn't see the reason why Chiclet would feel a need for protection.

"It's not for you and me, Tillie. It's for the young girls. But how can we get them to go if we won't?"

Every Wednesday night, we had our class. Looking at the class, you might feel that there was a reason for our record ten years. The young pretty ones never did join.

One little lady used to come out who really enjoyed it. She was plump, and middle-aged, and had six kids, all very polite. They all called her Mama, so pretty soon we did too. She didn't really seem to fit into a self-defence course, but then I don't know if any of us were what you'd expect. There was Edna, for example. In seven years, I have never seen Edna without curlers in her hair. Who she's curling it for, I don't know. Day or night, rain or shine, out shopping or at parties, Edna wears curlers. I even heard that her youngest surprised her one day when she was washing her hair, and started to cry. He didn't recognize her.

I guess that's why the men thought the class was funny. It was like locking the barn door after the horse was stolen.

We had been lucky enough to get a huge policeman to

teach the course, and to practise on. He was very patient with us, luckily, because nine of us had a problem. We were afraid we'd hurt him. We knew this was ridiculous but the knowledge didn't help. We just couldn't throw ourselves into it, except for Mama. She'd attack him with gusto, and every time she scored a direct hit, she'd snicker gleefully. It was cute.

When the attacks began in the project, we weren't too concerned. The first victim was Chiclet's husband, King Kong. He was dropping in to spy on Chiclet, and he had cut through the back.

"I was just walking along, and suddenly this midget jumped out at me. He was wearing a cape, for God's sake, and a hood, and he had a big "W" on his stomach. It was purple. He kicked me in the kneecap and ran away. And he laughed - this horrible little snigger. I don't know what for. I was never mean to a midget in my life. Honest."

Nobody really believed him.

Then there was another victim. Sam Grocholski, from next door. He never bothers anyone except his wife. Her, he figures he has a licence to maim. He was coming back from the beer parlour one night, and the Masked Snickerer got him too.

"You all know me. I'm a good neighbour. I work hard all day, I got a right to a beer or two at night. So how come, I'm walking home, minding my own business, and this strange little squirt jumps out at me. Look at this. He bit me. Right on the elbow. Then he ran off, laughing, like."

The attacks continued. Always on married men. The wives thought it was funny.

"You must have done *something*, Harry. Look what they say when a woman gets raped. Are you sure you didn't swagger, or something?"

The men started to talk about vigilante action. All the men attacked were rotten husbands. Chiclet and I sensed a pattern.

"Tillie, I'm worried. Someone could get hurt. Let's disband the class, and use them to keep an eye on the vigilantes."

For a week and a half, nothing happened. The ladies started to show up late for their shift, and then they stopped turning up at all. Chiclet and I hung in there, though. Finally, our patience was rewarded. We lurked, shivering, in Mug Alley. We had named the unlighted path joining the community some years ago in a burst of defiance against the Housing Authority when we found it was on their maps as Buttercup Lane. Now it appeared our chickens were coming home to roost.

"Hist!"

"WHAT!!!"

"Oh, Tillie, you've scared whoever it was..."

"Who the Hell is that?" asked a deep voice from somewhere in the region of where my right ear would be if I were three feet taller, and not crouched over. A flashlight beam caught me in the pith helmet and moved down.

"It's just Chiclet and Tillie. What are you two crazy females doing here? You could get hurt." Suddenly, Mug Alley was full of men, all telling us to go home where we belonged, and leave the rough stuff to them.

"We can take care of ourselves. We've had self-defence," said Chiclet freezingly.

A small scuffle broke out down the alley, followed by a male yip, a male curse, and masked snicker.

"Here he is! There he goes! Get out of my way, Chiclet! Watch out, Tillie! Where is he? Which way did he go?"

"There he goes! Down Elm Street!"

"Thanks, Tillie. Go home, now." Off they pounded, cursing, panting and limping.

"Shall we?" asked Chiclet.

"Let's", said I.

"Chiclet! Tillie! How nice of you to drop in. I'll make

76

some tea, as soon as I get rid of this cape."

"How are things going, Mama?"

"Not too bad, dear. Of course, I miss our lessons together. What's next on the programme?"

"I don't know, Mama. What do you think the ladies would like to learn?"

"Well, dear, I've been giving a lot of thought to Kung Fu."

"Uh.. I don't think so, Mama. Look, Mama, these midnight raids have got to stop. The vigilantes almost got you tonight. Why are you doing it?"

"Why Chiclet! You said ours was a common fight, and it was up to each of us to do something in our own small way and I never was much good at public speaking."

"Love your costume, Mama. Where did you get it?"

"Oh, thank you, Tillie. I made it myself at night school, in the sewing class. You know, as I got older, I started to take more and more night school classes, but then I realized I never got to use what I learned. So, when I started the self-defence classes, I asked myself 'Why not?'"

"Look, Mama, if we found some other way you could use what you learned, would you hang up your cape for good?"

"Oh, I think so, dear. I got most of the worst offenders anyway. More tea?"

Chiclet and I wrote down all that Mama had learned in her years of night school, and the next morning we went to see the Mayor. He saw us coming, and ducked into the men's room. This didn't bother Chiclet. She knew he had to come out sometime, so we just hung around. We got some funny looks, but Chiclet just gave some freezing ones in exchange. Finally, he emerged.

"Mr. Mayor, I hear you're setting up a Women's Bureau at City Hall. Is that true?"

"Oh, hello Chiclet," he said weakly, "Hello Tillie.

Yes, it's true, but.."

"Relax, Mr. Mayor. We didn't come to apply for the job. As you know, we're running for your job next time..that is, one of us is. We just came to recommend someone. She speaks three languages, types, knows bookkeeping, and is quiet and ladylike. How about it?"

Mama got an interview, and the Mayor liked her. After a while, he thought it was his own idea to hire her. So far, the men in our community believe that they scared away the ferocious midget who was attacking them. A lot of the women are puzzled about how a sweet little lady like Mama can hold down such a tough job. It did cross my mind when I noticed the Mayor limping last week...but I'm sure he'd rather have Mama on the payroll than me and my friend Chiclet.

SOME PEOPLE HAVE NO SENSE OF HUMOUR

Don't ever tell a joke to a psychiatrist or a social worker. They think jokes are symptoms.

A couple of months ago, Chiclet was in financial difficulties. Her fridge and stove quit at the same time. Then her washer started eating socks, a sure sign that it was in its death throes, too. She called her social worker. This is something one does not do lightly. If you're in luck when you're on Mothers' Allowance, years can go by without ever seeing one. But this was an emergency.

The next thing I knew, I got a phone call. "Tillie, I'm in the psychiatric ward. You've got to help me. The staff in here is nuts."

"What about the patients?"

"Oh, they're all right."

I went down to find out what had happened. Chiclet was grim.

"I just lost my cool. I got a new social worker. A man. He told me that anything he could do in his power to help me, he would, but I couldn't get a stove and a fridge and a washer all the same month. So I got sarcastic. I said 'Get me my inheritance'."

"Inheritance?"

"Oh, you know. I told you about Uncle Pi dying, and leaving me some money, along with all the other nephews and nieces. I figure it should come to about two hundred. But then I realized I shouldn't have told him."

She was right. The thing is, the province considers its support a loan, payable any time you have money, so it's always best to keep quiet about winning at bingo, or finally getting some alimony, or whatever. So when she realized what she had said, she told him she was just joking. The next thing she knew, she was in the hospital. Once she got there, they began asking her about her inheritance, and how much she thought she was getting. The thing was, if she told them, Welfare would take it, and Chiclet didn't want that.

"Let them find their own uncle." Gradually, they got off the topic of inheritances, and on to others.

"I saw the psychiatrist this morning, Tillie. He said, 'What's bothering you, Ms. Gomez?' So I told him. I said, 'My fridge and stove and washer are all broken. I have three kids to feed and keep clean, and I don't have any money.'"

"And?"

"He said, 'We all have financial problems, Ms. Gomez. What's really bothering you?' He wanted to know all about my sex life."

"What did you do?"

"What else? I lied."

Well, we decided that the rest couldn't do any harm, and I offered to watch Chiclet's kids while she planned how to get out. We decided it was probably the same system as usual — like jail or school. Just play possum, be polite, and get out.

We were wrong.

After studying the situation, Chiclet reported that we had it all backwards. "You have to do something strange, Tillie. Then they figure you've got it out of your system, and you can leave."

So we began to plan what Chiclet could do to convince them that she had snapped — safely. She began going to occupational therapy. She painted a thing that gave me the shivers. It was a satanic face, with a background of people burning at the stake. When I visited her the next time, it was gone.

"What happened?"

"I told you the staff is crazy. The therapist came in and asked me what it was. I told her, people burning at the stake. 'Ah', she says, 'a barbecue.' She asked me if she could hang it in the staff room."

Strike one.

I was getting worried about Chiclet. The place was making her uneasy. It looked bright and cheerful enough, but there was an orderly who kept trying to interest her in buying a plaster of Paris breast from his brother-in-law, even though she had two perfectly good ones of her own. He also kept sneaking up behind her and touching her. And now I noticed that she opened the bathroom door by standing a few feet away from it, and poking it with something.

"What are you doing?"

"Tillie, that's the only place you can ever be alone here. I always wonder if someone has committed suicide in there."

She's right. There's always someone hanging around keeping an eye on everybody. I found myself starting to open the doors like that, too, although the only thing I ever discovered in there was a nude male sitting on the edge of the bathtub singing "Shoo Fly Pie and Apple Pan Dowdy."

We had to get her out. We decided she should hit somebody. An expression of violence should do it. But who? We didn't want to hurt anybody. We decided on a big male nurse. Chiclet couldn't possibly hurt him; he was built like a steel door. But it should get the idea across. The next day, I went to see her.

"Well?"

"I tried, Tillie. But I couldn't do it. I wasn't mad at him, and he just stood there, looking like Jerome the Giraffe."

Strike two.

By this time, we decided that those who looked normal stayed in forever, while those who looked weird got out. So Chiclet started walking around, wearing sunglasses indoors, loudly spouting this crazy Spanish poetry, all about if I am pink, then you're blue, and together we can have a violet time, or something like that. They decided she had a literary flair, and put her in charge of the ward newspaper.

Things got worse. She tried to be funny again, and made some joke about an argument in the ward over whether to paint the wall Jung yellow or Freudian purple. Down to the psychiatrist's office to discuss why she associated purple with Freud.

"Doesn't everyone?"

"Chiclet. We agreed. No more jokes, right? They do not have a sense of humour. We may never get you out of here now."

Our last bet was a temper tantrum, or a fit of hysterics, or something to convince the powers that she had it (whatever) safely out of her system. I went in, and reminded Chiclet of every rotten thing that had ever happened to her. I also put her hair in curlers. This causes her eyes to water, and I figured it would given her a head start. Then I went to find the head nurse. After all, it wouldn't be any good without a witness.

"Nurse, could you come down to room 14 for a moment, please? Ms. Gomez seems to be very upset."

"Mrs. Gomez? Oh, surely not Mrs. Gomez. She's my favourite patient. What's wrong? Oh, Mrs. Gomez, dear, don't cry. You'll get me all upset too." The head nurse promptly burst into tears. This was not working out at all. Chiclet pulled herself together and started to calm the nurse down.

Strike three.

I was now so depressed I could have done with a rest too. "I give up, Chiclet. I don't know how we're going to spring you."

I went home very discouraged. Chiclet is an organizer. I decided she had organized the psychiatric ward. No wonder they didn't want her to go. We didn't either.

To my surprise, I got a call the next morning from Chiclet. She was home.

"How did you do it?"

"I really did snap, Tillie. My psychiatrist sent me a message. He said I had to stop going barefoot in the ward, and wear shoes, and that I should try to dress 'femininely'. I stomped in there, and told him it was none of his bloody business how I dressed, and I was fed up with him poking into my sex life. I told him that I was through talking to him. I said if he didn't let me alone I would put a curse on him."

"And he let you out just like that? You didn't really put a curse on him, did you?" I didn't really believe in Chiclet's curses, but I didn't disbelieve in them either. She never threatened to put one on unless she was really mad.

"I didn't have to. He said he liked spunk. I was now cured, he said. So he called the nurse, and told her to discharge me."

When Chiclet got home, she found a cheque for two hundred and five dollars waiting for her. She got a new second-hand fridge and stove, and Welfare came through with enough to fix her washer. The social worker came by, and told her the rest had done her a world of good. He was very pleased with himself. He said there were a couple of other clients he was going to try to get admitted for a rest.

I was very proud of Chiclet. She didn't say a word.

IN SEARCH OF A PORTFOLIO

Chiclet and I were waiting at the airport for our plane to leave, and already I was having second thoughts. Neither of us had flown before, and I was a little jittery. Chiclet, of course, was being cool. She looked like an old hand, and was not only working at calming me down, but had taken several strangers in tow also. What were two public housing tenants doing, waiting for a plane to take them halfway across the country?

Well, Chiclet always figures there's nowhere to go but up. I guess it's all in the way you look at things. Some people would be more likely to say "That's it..I've hit bottom.. I'm finished." Not Chiclet. She says, "Look at all the possibilities there are." Political life is one of the possibilities she sees before her. There's never been a woman prime minister, or governor general, so she figures there might be an opening there for her. Of course, she realizes she can't start at the top.

So there we were in the airport off to a political convention as delegates for our area. This had taken a lot of wangling. We also had to do a lot of brushing up on which political party stood for what.

Chiclet has never been on record as favouring the present government. But then, she's never been on record as favouring any government. She figures any of them could use some improvement. As a matter of fact, what she'd really like to see is some sort of coalition, with all the absolute twits left out. She figures there might be enough politicians left over to form a government. Of course, none of the parties agree with this idea. It seems a certain number of twits are absolutely necessary. We haven't yet figured out why.

We've been disillusioned about government since we met an M.P. for the first time. The first MP we happened to meet was our very own member. Further encounters with him have not improved the situation. We can't figure out how he could hold down any job, much less an elected one.

"They say people get the government they deserve, Tillie. What does that say about us?"

"We didn't vote for him."

"Obviously, that's not enough. If we don't want him elected again, we shall have to take steps."

There were two ways we could take steps. We could join the riding association of the party he belonged to, and try to get someone else elected, or we could join a different party's riding association, and work against the whole party. We tried sounding out the local riding association in his party. We found out why he was so well-beloved. He used the "old neighbourhood boy" approach. Actually, he hadn't been seen in our area of the city since some time in the depression. But he owned property there — slum property. He gave us the line which we were to discover was a common one among politicians. He could understand our needs, he told us, because he had been poor once. In fact, he used to have to go to school barefoot.

After we had been around for a while politically, we were forced to assume that there had been no shoe industry in the country until after the 1940's. How is it that we were never informed of this fact in school?

We realized that there was no point in trying to get his own party to replace him. We would have to go to another party, and hope that their candidate was young enough not to have a fixation with the shoe crisis of the earlier part of the century, and able to deal with the more up-to-date crisis facing us now.

The opposing camp was delighted to see us. They had all sorts of room for envelope-lickers. In spite of the fact that we were unskilled at politics, we felt that this was a comedown. It wasn't that licking envelopes was so bad once you got used to tasting peppermint glue all day long, but when you're slotted in a position like that, nobody listens to your advice. We had thought this candidate might like our advice on how to approach our fellow public housing tenants. He didn't. He already had advice on this subject from other advisors, and their advice was "don't".

"Those people are dangerous."

"Bosh. Chiclet is as dangerous as we come, and she has yet to mug a political candidate."

"Oh, Tillie. You and Chiclet are... well... different."

"Different? We're women. We're heads of households. We're unemployed. We don't have any money. We're about as different as Tweedle Dum from Tweedle Dee."

Of course, that's not what he meant. He meant he knew us. We didn't mug people. Therefore he assumed not that in general we didn't mug people, as we had hoped, but that Chiclet and I were not typical. Nothing could convince our dauntless hero that he would be perfectly safe in our areas. He wouldn't come. That's when Chiclet and I began to realize why our people had such an exaggerated idea of politicians and their rationality. Familiarity breeds contempt.

More in sorrow than in anger, Chiclet and I resigned

our positions as envelope lickers, and trotted over to the third party in our area. This party didn't seem to stand a chance. Naturally, for that reason, they were running a young female as their candidate. It really seems as if women never get to run unless it looks hopeless anyway. Of course, if by some fluke they win, they get to keep the riding. They were so desperate here that they actually welcomed our advice.

When election came, we didn't win the riding of course. Our "old neighbourhood boy" did, but we took all the public housing polls, and our people came out to vote in bigger numbers than they had in the last twenty-five years, so we were definitely persona grata. That's how come we were getting to go to a convention.

Chiclet figured that since this party was at the bottom, there was nowhere to go but up, and when it got there, she would be right in there as Minister of Finance, or something. We had hopes because we had noted that new ministers never know anything about the jobs they get.

"See?" Chiclet said, "I'd be perfect for Finance Minister. If there's anything I don't know, that's it."

This had sounded fine to me on the ground. Once we were in the air, however, all kinds of doubts came flooding in. I didn't have much time to consider them, however, as I was convinced that all that was keeping the plane aloft was my personal faith in it, so I had to keep my thoughts busy on how much I trusted the plane.

Chiclet ruined her pose of the well-travelled blasé flyer by devouring all her food when it came. We had both heard absolutely terrible stories about the food one gets served on the national airline, so we were ready to be revolted. We thought it was absolutely delicious, and we didn't have to cook it, and it didn't cost extra. We ate every crumb.

"Tch! Steak again," we heard someone murmur.

"Tillie, aren't you utterly bored with steak?"

"Oh, indubitably. This business of having it regularly every five years does terrible things to my insides."

We were still giggling when the airplane landed and we got out. A different city, in a different province! Of course, all we could see was a few trees and the air terminal so far, but things would look up.

We never got to see any more trees, or the new city, or the new province, and we hardly ate or slept. We had a marvelous time. We talked, and argued, and watched all the slickies, because some day we're going to be slickies too. Right before we accept our portfolios.

HAVE I GOT A PICTURE FOR YOU

Chiclet and I were suffering from a real fit of depression. Here we were, still. We seemed to have been running for years, like the White Queen, just to stay in place. After all our work, what had happened, really? We were still unemployed. Or we were again unemployed. The future looked bleak. I was heading into a period where I would be less employable than ever, because of my age, and Chiclet's employment record served only to arouse a snicker at the Manpower offices. Could it be that we were doing something wrong?

We began to roll the years back, in our minds, and review all the schemes we had tried to better ourselves. Some of them had been pretty good.

We decided that we were much more talented than we appeared on the surface. The only problem was to convince a prospective employer of this. We decided to try writing up a resumé for each of us. We got as far as age, name, marital status, and then we started to draw a blank. We didn't want to put down education, because this is where we always got sunk. Formal education, that is. Chiclet and I had been learning at a remarkable rate since we got together, but how to express this so it sounded impressive? How about starting with community work. Unlike when we first started working in the community, this now seemed to be quite a respectable way to get started in the work force.

Linda Cunningham came in. "Hi. What are you doing?"

"We're trying to capitalize on our work skills."

"What does that mean?"

"We're drawing up a list of things we know how to do."

Chiclet said "It's really pretty good, Linda. Look, we know how to chair a meeting, we know all about parliamentary procedure.."

"I don't," I said firmly. "I can never remember what a point of order is."

"Tillie, you know very well that's only used by nitpickers, anyway. We know how to draw up an agenda, how to take minutes, how to work on committees, how to keep track of petty cash.."

"Let's not get carried away, Chiclet. You may know how to manage petty cash, but I get hopelessly fouled up, and you know it."

"Never mind. We know how to work videotape equipment, tape recorders typewriters, copiers."

"I don't think an employer is going to be impressed by twenty-five words a minute, Chiclet. And you forgot to put in that I can't use a business phone. All those flashing lights paralyze me. I just panic, and press the first button handy."

"Tillie, think positively. Don't start thinking about what you don't know how to do, start thinking about what you know how to do. We've had experience on the air..that's it! That's what we'll do. We'll be reporters." Once Chiclet has something firmly in mind, there's no way to dislodge it. In her mind, we were now Crusading Reporters, and all that remained was to get hired.

90

"Chiclet, we didn't go to journalism school. What makes you think anyone would hire us?"

"We'll produce a documentary, and sell it."

Linda thought this was a marvellous idea, and she and Chiclet began discussing subject matter.

"I hate to throw cold water on this, but where are we going to get the equipment?"

"Oh, Tillie. We'll borrow a videotape recorder from a university, or somewhere, and when we sell the show, we can pay for the tapes."

That was it. Chiclet began to phone around, to borrow the equipment, and I went home to feed my kids and to wonder if she really had something there. After all, why not? We weren't getting anywhere following the usual route, and time was of the essence.

The next morning, bright and early, Chiclet phoned. "It's here, Tillie. Come on over, and we'll work out a script." When I got there, Chiclet was sitting in a lawn chair. It had *Ms. Gomez, Director* painted in large letters on the back.

Now all we had to do was discover, somewhere in the city, a story no one else was covering. Of course, it also had to be timely, and interesting.

"Tillie, I think it should be a heartwarming story."

"A boy and his dog?"

"There's no need to be sarcastic. Maybe we should do one about pets. We've got a real problem here with animals. Let's go out and see how many strays we can find."

On any normal day of the week, a brisk walk will turn up two or three animals which look as if, with the slightest encouragement, they'll follow you home. Over the years, my children have brought home a turtle, a frog, twenty or thirty cats and dogs, and one pedestrian budgie, who was striding along the middle of the road, so intent on where he was going he failed to see a car bearing down on him. It missed him, but he became overcome by the gasoline fumes, and keeled over. My daughter brought him home. Although he was able to fly, he preferred to walk everywhere he went. I remembered how miners used to bring canaries down in the mines, and were warned of bad air when the birds passed out. I thought we could use our budgie as a pollution index, but the cat had other plans. Not wanting to have a domestic tragedy on my hands, I had given him away. Actually, we had had so many tragedies, it was embarrassing when the Housing Authority came around to landscape, and turned up a regular pet cemetary in our back yard.

However, look as we might, we found no strays that day. We regrouped at noon. By this time, we had attracted quite a following. One little kid kept trying to get us to do a story on his caterpillar, but we felt it would be of limited interest. Although we had found no strays, we had found all kinds of signs. One area I visited had obviously hosted a large party of dogs at a recent time. I nervously checked the soles of my shoes.

Chiclet lounged in her chair and frowned. "We'll have to start shooting today. I promised to turn back the equipment in three days, and we can't afford to waste time."

"Maybe we should have worked out the script first."

"Well, we'll have to do the best we can. Why not film here? We can take some footage of kids in the back yard, it's always swarming with them, and maybe we can do a documentary on the lack of recreation equipment in public housing."

At this point, several spectators excused themselves. "Lunch" I thought vaguely, and went home to feed the kids.

When we assembled in the back yard, a surprise awaited us. Out of her door emerged Poison Ivy's daughter, a kid who always seemed to be running in the house with a bleeding knee. She walked slowly toward us, dressed to kill, and gave a polite smile. Three little boys who usually have a fight going between at least two of them, were sedately pulling each other in a wagon, their freshly-combed hair gleaming wetly. The only children who looked normal were ours, and compared to the others, they looked degenerate. We took some pictures, to show that all this effort had not been wasted, but we were getting discouraged.

One unexpected by-product of the filming was the quiet in the back yard for the next couple of days, but it was discouraging. It's hard to be inconspicuous when you're loaded down with about fifty pounds of gear, and the director is running around madly, yelling "Pan! Pan!" Wearing a borrowed pith helmet and swinging a riding crop dangerously.

I got some interesting cloud patterns and a close-up of Georgia Wiseman's toenails as she lay sunbathing. I also got some caterpillar shots, because a kid kept running in front of the camera, waving one about, and I got a lot of footage of feet, from when I thought the camera was off.

When it came time to turn in the equipment, we were discouraged again. However, the cable station was kind enough to run the film during a vacant half hour, and called it "Summer Fun", and Chiclet is now busy writing a script for a feature film about the effect of commercials on the home. She figures if everyone is going to look like a toothpaste ad when we film them, there must be some way to use it. She's applying for a Canada Council grant under the name Cinema Public, and we're going to co-direct.

But this time I get to wear the pith helmet. Now if I only knew where I could get a monocle.....

UNLEASED PASSION

We have two kinds of men in our communities – the ones who officially live there, and the ones who aren't on the lease. The ones who officially live there have a pretty busy time of it. When they're home they're kept hopping. Most of them have jobs that pretty well wipe them out physically, so it's hard to get their help for anything, unless it's automobiles.

Most of the women don't know much about cars, except that they either run or they don't. If they run, fine. If they don't, then you have to find a man. The men get dragged out of bed or off the couch every time there's a dead battery or a flat tire. They enjoy it though. All the rest of the men come out and join them, and they hold a consultation on the patient. Most of them have their own favourite tools that they use, and they'll send the kids back to the house to get them. Then they'll have a long discussion about which instruments to use for surgery. If it's major surgery, they can enjoy themselves for a week.

If a single woman wants a man to do something for her, she has to be pretty sneaky. If she just goes to the

94

door and asks, he's bound to be too tired. For instance, when Linda Cunningham wanted to buy Chiclet's old refrigerator, we had to figure out how to get it from Chiclet's to Linda's. Chiclet's ex-husband, King Kong, was over at Chiclet's with his cousin, Fat Freddie. King Kong was trying to make Chiclet jealous by describing the girl he was taking out, and Fat Freddie was ogling Linda.

"How'd you guys like to get this fridge over to Linda's?"

They quickly remembered a prior engagement. Chiclet looked out in the yard. Not a man was in sight.

"Well, if we can get it out to the back yard between the three of us we'll be all right."

"But Chiclet, it's still three blocks to my place."

"Tillie, you and Linda take the bottom."

We staggered down the hall, and out the back door. By the time we got there, we were shaking.

"Hey, Chiclet! Where you taking that fridge?" Mr. Grocholski suddenly appeared in the door.

"Just over to Linda's."

By this time, a few men had appeared.

"You don't think you're going to make it all the way there?"

"Chiclet," I said, "let's ask them to carry it."

"Sure we are. Why not? (Shut up Tillie. They'll just say they're too tired.)"

"The three of you can't carry that. You need a man to help you. Too bad you don't have one."

"Who needs men? We can do it just fine, and probably better than you could."

In two minutes, we had that fridge over at Linda's, with all the men trying to prove how fast they could do it. We had to admit that they had done it faster than we could have, and they went home happy, figuring they'd put us in our place.

The same thing happened when we tried to get them

to coach a baseball team. They were too tired. So Chiclet decided to coach. Every time she was out there, a few kibitzers would turn up and tell her what she was doing wrong. Finally they took pity on the kids, and took over. It was a good thing, because Chiclet doesn't know a baseball from a football.

We never ask the unofficial men to help out, because officially they're invisible. There's a sort of Ladies' Agreement about them. If I go over to Linda's to visit, and there's a man in her living room, I pretend I just came over to ask her something, and go away.

The only thing that sometimes threatens to upset the cart is the kids. Some of them are so thrilled that they go door-to-door. "There's a man in our house, Mrs. Gomez. Hello, Tillie. Guess what? There's a man in our house." Or else they will walk right up to the poor schnook and ask "Are you going to marry our mother?"

We have one woman in the project who's an incurable snoop. She's always trying to find out what's going on, and making wild guesses when she can't find out, and starting rumours. Her name's Ivy. Naturally, we call her Poison Ivy. Poison Ivy is the only one the kids never tell about their mothers' visitors. She runs out and collars them, and says "Who's that man I saw going in your house?"

"What man?"

Ivy is short, and when she's on the trail of something, or thinks she is, her nose quivers. It's not an endearing trait. She is particularly anxious to root out sin, because, of course, Ivy's union is legally blessed.

Ivy's husband is the most browbeaten little man you ever saw. He goes off to work, comes home and does the housework. Then he puts the kids to bed, and then he works in the garden. He doesn't say boo to a goose.

One time, Chiclet and Linda and I were particularly mad at Ivy. She had spread a rumour that Mrs. Grocholski, one of the teetotallers we have in the project, was a secret drinker. Then she tried to whip up a sympathetic reaction to poor King Kong, by saying that Chiclet had thrown him out surrounded by green garbage bags, as if she was putting out trash. This last rumour was infuriating because it was true. Chiclet had never been anywhere, so she had no suitcases. She had packed all his clothes in garbage bags. A couple of days later, one of her kids was putting out the garbage, and Ivy asked him if he'd been thrown out too.

So we decided to start a rumour that her husband was really Igor Gouzenko, and the only reason he got to stay in the country was because he'd agreed to marry Ivy. We didn't though. After all, we'd never heard him say a word, and we hadn't seen him in a pillow case. Maybe he was.

There's nothing worse than a rumour which turns out to be true.

DISCOVERIES

Everybody knew Shaughnessy was a bad egg. You could tell just by looking at him. He had red hair and freckles, and a mischievous look on his face, and he was eighteen. And he had short hair.

He turned up at Chiclet's door about a year ago. Her first reaction was "Out!"

"Now, wait a minute, Chiclet."

"Ms. Gomez to you, Twerp."

"All right then, Ms. Gomez. What have you got against me?"

"Shaughnessy, I know your kind. There isn't one good, honest thing about you."

"Chi..Ms. Gomez, Have I ever done anything, to your personal knowledge, to hurt anyone in this community? Or is it my face?"

"Your face?"

"I know what I look like. 'With a face like that', they say, 'what can you expect?' But I thought that you would give me a chance to prove them wrong."

"Well.. come in."

Did I also mention that Shaughnessy was smart? He

98

knew Chiclet's weak spot. He had suddenly transformed himself into the underdog. So for weeks we heard nothing but stories about 'poor misunderstood Eric'. We tried to reason with her.

"Tillie, are you going to tell me 'there's no smoke without fire'? Or 'you can tell a book by its cover' or one of those old chestnuts? Because if you are, you're not the person I thought you were. This poor kid has been discriminated against just because he has short hair and *looks* like he's up to something. We owe him a chance."

"Why us, Chiclet? He's not one of our kids, he didn't grow up here, he's just a hangeron. Anyway, he's not a kid, he's eighteen."

"Tillie, that's the trouble with the world. 'He's not one of us. Why should we help him?' Do you realize that you sound like a bigot?"

Well, that got me. What did I know about Eric the Red? True, nothing good. But on the other hand, nothing bad either. Just rumours. Maybe Chiclet was right. Who wants to look like a bigot? So, it became customary for the three of us to spend our evenings hanging around Chiclet's, after the kids were in bed, singing while Eric played his guitar. He played all the good tunes – "Blowing in the Wind" and "Bobbie McGee", and sometimes really old ones, like "The Four Marys". He had a beautiful voice.

One evening he turned up with his guitar and a suitcase. "This is the last time I'll be here. Tillie, Chiclet, I'm going to miss you. You're the only people I care about. But I've got to go. I'm being evicted."

"But where will you go? What will you do? Have you got any money?"

"Oh, don't worry about me...I'll manage somehow..."

Of course, the upshot was that he spent the night on Chiclet's couch. One of the rules that the Housing

Authority has is that nobody but the immediate family is to live in the housing they so kindly provide us with.

"Rules are made to be broken," said Chiclet. "Who are they to say I can't have an overnight guest?"

I couldn't argue with that. But I felt a little uneasy. For one thing, I knew what the neighbours would think. And say. But I knew better than to mention it to Chiclet. If I did, she'd keep him forever. The next day, she told me that Eric was going to stay with her until he found a place.

"Chiclet, I've got a teenager. Don't get mad, but set some rules. Only feed him three times a day. Don't let him have his friends in unless you're there. Make him pay something for his room and board. If he can't pay money, make him clean the house or babysit or something. Don't give him a free ride."

"He's a guest, not a boarder. Don't be silly."

"Chiclet, honest, I know kids. Don't.."

"He's not a kid."

This looked like a good time to go home, so I did. My suspicions, which had been lulled to sleep to the strains of guitar music, suddenly woke up. Eric must have had prior notice of his eviction. You don't just get thrown out on your ear without warning. He probably knew for a month, or at least a week. Had he been setting Chiclet up? Had he been evicted at all? What could he be after? None of us had anything of value as far as money went. Chiclet's home is lovely, but that's colour sense and imagination, not money. The old phrase "after the spoons" drifted through my mind, but I knew better. In our neighbourhood, the place to be after the spoons is outside in the spring, when melting snow reveals all last year's spoon harvest waiting to be collected. The kids smuggle them outside in the summer to make mud pies with. That's our recreation programme. What could he want? Obviously, nothing. I was being nasty and suspicious.

Week followed week, and still Eric showed no sign of leaving. He ordered Chiclet's kids around and she let him! One afternoon when I went over, Chiclet was alone in the house, and depressed.

"What's the matter? Has King Kong been hassling you again?"

King Kong was Chiclet's husband, gone but not forgotten. He took care of that by dropping over on a surprise basis to hassle her, sending relatives over with propaganda about good women obeying their husbands, and so on. He wasn't really a bad soul – just the usual ex-husband — dumb, overbearing, musclebound, conceited and generally unpleasant. You know – the kind you tend to marry if you marry when you're sixteen.

"Who? Oh, George. No."

"George. Is that what his name was? Listen Chiclet, what's wrong? You're not acting naturally."

"Tillie, I'm in trouble. I owe two months back rent. How am I going to raise that kind of money?"

"Chiclet! You? You always say.."

"Tillie. I know what I always say. That doesn't help."

Money. If we knew anything about raising money, there wouldn't be any public housing. We were always trying to think of ways to raise money. None of them ever worked.

"Tillie. I'll have to get a job."

Work? Chiclet had got married at sixteen, and spent the rest of her fairly short life raising kids. For those who don't think that is work, let them try it. However, it pays zilch as money goes.

"Chiclet, what can you do that's marketable? You can't type. You don't have a degree. You'll have to pay a babysitter to watch your kids, you'll have to have clothes, bus fare, lunch money, pantyhose. Do you know how much it costs to keep a working woman in pantyhose alone? You can't afford to work."

"Tillie, I asked for help, not defeatism. There must be something I can do, I did used to have a job, before I got married."

"Yeah, but there's no demand around here for a girl that turns into a gorilla."

Now I hadn't intended to imply that Chiclet has no talents. She does. She's one of the leaders in our community. When something needs fixing Chiclet gets it done. When somebody's in trouble, Chiclet's there. However, nobody pays for that kind of work either.

"How did you get in such a fix?"

"Well, food costs are going up, and.." she trailed off weakly. Trailing off anything weakly is not like Chiclet.

"It's Eric the Red. He's been eating you out of house and home, borrowing money, never paying it back. He's a parasite."

"Oh, Tillie, it's nothing like that. It's just he's needed bus fare to go and look for work, and he does eat a lot, but I'm glad to do it. Somebody has to take care of boys like that."

I didn't like it. Oh, not just that Chiclet was in debt to the Housing Authority, although that worried me, because I figured if there was anybody they'd like to get rid of, it was Chiclet. Mainly, though, I didn't like it because Chiclet wasn't herself. Her ordinary self, if she got into financial trouble, would phone the Housing Authority and tell them to keep their pants on, she wasn't leaving town, and she'd pay them when she could.

"Is that all that's bothering you Chiclet?"

I didn't get an answer, because just then Eric came in flung himself down in a chair, and said "How about a cup of tea?"

Chiclet got up to get it. Not knowing Chiclet, you may not see the significance in this. Let me give you a hint. When her five year old would say "Can I have a glass of milk?" she'd say, "Sure honey, you know where

102

it is." Her belief was that mothers shouldn't become servants or waitresses to their kids; it wasn't good for them or her.

I went home.

A few nights later, she called me at about 2 a.m. After I got over the panic induced by having the phone ring in the middle of the night, which to me always means Birth or Death or Trouble, I threw on an overcoat and ran over.

She was herself again. "I threw the twerp out! Tillie, do you know what he did?"

"What?"

"He followed me up to my bedroom."

"Chiclet..he didn't try...I mean, are you all right?"

"No, it wasn't like that. It was worse. He acted like he was doing me a favour, like he owed it to me. It made me feel...old, unwanted. It made me feel Married. It was horrible."

"What did you do?"

"Suddenly a voice inside me said 'You! Dummy! What the Hell's the matter with you? This kid comes along, you know he's no good, you take him in, you feed him, you let him use you every other way, what did you expect? Kick him out!' So I did."

"Did he just go? Just like that?"

"Well, no. He yelled a little, said I must be frigid, or a lesbian..you know that old line."

"What did you do then?"

"I told him I did have a hang-up. I preferred to wait till males grew up, and he'd better leave while he still had the chance. He threw a few things, and kicked the door, but he left. What a relief."

"So, what now?"

"First thing in the morning I'm scrubbing the house, then I'm taking the kids out for Chinese food, then I'm phoning the Housing Authority to tell them to shut up, they'll get their money. Tillie, I had an awfully close call."

"Oh, come on, Chiclet. After three kids? I mean, you're not exactly.."

"I didn't mean my purity, you nut. I meant my self-respect. I was born a virgin, it didn't do me any good, and when I lost it, it was no big deal. But I worked hard for my self-respect."

Well, I knew I didn't trust Shaughnessy. Still, if you'd asked me, I wouldn't have said he was more than a sneak thief — I thought spoons would probably be his limit. But Self-Respect — that would be grand theft. Hard to prove, though. Once you've lost it, how do you prove you've ever had it?

CAMP CHICLET

"I need a vacation," said Chiclet. "I'm getting crabby with my neighbours, and yelling at their kids, and yelling at my kids. I've got to get away."

"Where can you go, Chiclet?" asked Linda.

I didn't bother to say anything. This is our yearly rebellion. Every year, when summer comes, and five hundred kids explode into the back-yard, the immediate impulse is flight. But Linda was right. Where was there to go?

Last year, Linda went to a "Family Camp" that one of the local church groups sponsored, and came back in worse shape than she was in when she left. "It was terrible. The water suddenly got deep where the bottom dropped away, there were sharp rocks, we were near a provincial highway — everywhere I looked, it seemed more dangerous, and the trouble was, the kids weren't used to that kind of danger. I'd jump out of bed in the morning and count my kids, to make sure one of them hadn't left early and gone to the beach and drowned. We had corn on the cob every night for a week. I don't know if it was cheap last year, or what, but it sure played hob with my kids' digestion. And besides that, we were supposed to be grateful. I hate having to be grateful on cue, especially when it's for something I don't like."

One time, when I was looking in the phone book for something, I had come across an ad. "Get away from it all at Blind Bay Inn. Helicopter flights to the lodge." Ever since then, when things got black, Chiclet and I would say "It's time to go to Blind Bay." We had no idea where it was because somehow if we didn't know, it stayed inviolate. We figured if things ever really got terrible then we'd find out where it was. Until then, it was our secret. Of course, we knew we were fooling ourselves. For one thing, it would cost a fortune. For another, it would probably be full of men and guns and fishing rods, and be actively hostile to us. But the real facts about Blind Bay didn't matter. As long as we never went there, it could be anything we wanted.

But it wasn't working its magic this year. It really was time that we got away, but at the same time, getting away was an impossibility. Anyway, it wasn't just me and Chiclet and Linda who needed to get away. We were all at the edge of our patience, and what made it worse was that we knew there was no hope. Those of us who work never have a job long enough to qualify for a vacation, and being unemployed is not the same thing at all. Those of us on Mothers' Allowance certainly don't get vacation pay, either.

Edna had managed to get all her kids off to camp, which was nice for them, but the cost of getting them off, even though she had managed to get them subsidized (ugh!) was still astronomical. They each had to have so many pairs of pyjamas, so many pairs of socks, a raincoat, rubber boots, sweaters, a sleeping bag, hat, running shoes, and on and on, and they all had to be labelled. At home, the top and bottom half of the pyjamas don't have to match, even if you sleep at a

106

neighbour's, but for camp, everything has to be perfect, so they at least don't *look* subsidized. So Edna had a perfect opportunity to go away. All she lacked was money and a place to go.

"We ought to get a camp going for mothers."

I groaned. "Have you any idea how much work that would be? We'd have to find a place, and get the money for travel, and get a cook or something, and get baby-sitters for the mothers, and that's not even counting the administration."

"I don't care", Chiclet said. "We need it. Let's start figuring things out. Get a pencil, Tillie."

Chiclet began to divide up the work load. "I'll work on getting us a place. Linda, you go door-to-door and find out how many want to go. Tillie, which do you want to handle? Transportation or baby-sitters?"

"Transportation, I guess. It would be easier to get a whole train donated than baby-sitting. But I'm not starting till I find out how many want to go."

"Okay, Tillie. I'll get on it this afternoon," Linda said. "Do we just ask single parents, Chiclet?"

"No. A mother is a mother. Besides, maybe we won't have to get baby-sitters for the married ones. Maybe the husbands will sit."

In a pig's eye.

The idea of the mothers' camp was very popular. Linda found a hundred mothers who wanted to go.

"We'll have to divide it into periods. If we can get a campsite for a month, we could get twenty-five mothers a week up there. Tillie, try to get transportation for twenty-five."

Oh, sure. I might be able to get transportation for twenty-five once, one way, but this idea would need eight trips. Still I resolved to do my best. Maybe if I did a good job, I wouldn't have to do anything else. I had a horrible fear that I was going to end up cooking. I suddenly realized why the camp Linda went to had corn

107

on the cob every night. You didn't have to be able to cook to serve that.

"I got one! Listen, Tillie. If we wait till September we can have the Girl Guide camp. It's perfect. It's got cabins, bunks, a cook house, a lake — everything. And it's only thirty-five miles away."

"September — that's a long time off, Chiclet. And that'll mean that everyone's kids will be home. Everybody will need a baby-sitter."

"Yeah, but some of the kids will be at school — they won't need sitting from eight-thirty till four."

I could see some problems in this — at least if you baby-sit in the summer, you have some days where you can just stick a bathing suit on them, and send them off to play under the hose. School meant getting baby-sitters who could do laundry.

I managed to get a service club to donate the buses. It would have been a lot easier if we'd all been handicapped or senior citizens or something though. The man I talked to seemed to think it was immoral to want to get away from our kids. It seems to me that there are a whole lot of things that are immoral if you don't have money, but perfectly acceptable if you do.

Gradually the plans for the mothers' camp took shape, but we still didn't have the baby-sitter problem solved.

"Maybe we could do each other's. Like Tillie, you look after my kids the first week, and then when I come back, I'll look after yours so you can go."

"That's nice, Linda. What happens if you break your leg up there? Then I don't get to go. It's too risky. Anyway, after a whole summer of kids of my own at home, the last thing I need are more. No matter whose." Besides, I might be able to stomach Linda's kids, or Chiclet's, but I couldn't think of anybody who would voluntarily condemn themselves to a week with Poison Ivy's kids.

This looked like the rock we might flounder on. We

108

had managed to find a volunteer cook for the whole month. One of the students at the community college was going to do it, and get credits for it. Mrs. Rotardier, whose kids were all too big to require sitting, had volunteered to take the nursing duties up at the camp for a month, since she had been a nurse twenty-four years ago. We figured cuts and bruises probably hadn't changed all that much since then.

Finally, the week before the camp was due to start, we had things fairly well under control. Chiclet had got all the women on Mothers' Allowance doctor's certificates saying they needed a week's rest, so they got Visiting Homemakers. Forty women had dropped out, for one reason or another. Some husbands had not liked the idea of their wives getting away, especially if they hadn't been able to. Some of the women had new boyfriends, and didn't want to risk losing them. Mrs. Belanger had cracked up, and was spending her vacation in the psychiatric ward. The rest of us had to trade baby-sitting services.

The first fifteen women went up, and the rest of us waited feverishly to see if it was worth it. I was going on the second trip, so I was getting on the bus as Linda got off. I could tell just by looking at her. She looked five years younger.

The second day I was up there, two husbands and a boyfriend turned up to insist that their women go home and fulfill their wifely functions, but Chiclet handled that. When she got there, things looked pretty ugly. Somebody had pointed out that no men were allowed, and this had seemed like a direct challenge.

"Oh boys. I guess I was right all along, eh? I knew you couldn't cope by yourselves. Too much for you, wasn't it? Men just don't have the stamina women do, I guess. We spend three hundred and sixty-five days a year doing that stuff. We don't even get Sundays or Christmas off, but you couldn't even manage one week.

I guess it just goes to show you can dish it out, but you can't take it."

"We can so. We just came up to see what was going on."

After they left, we settled back into the camp routine. I had figured I was going to climb mountains, water ski, and diet.

I lay by the lake and ate for a whole week. I may not look five years younger, and I may be ten pounds heavier, but I don't care.

Next year, we're going to start planning in the winter, and maybe we can have two camps, one in May and one in September. I'm going again, even if I have to babysit Poison Ivy's kids.

NEXT DOOR NEIGHBOURS

"Chiclet, this is humiliating. I feel like a kept woman."

"That's the whole idea, Linda. Welfare is supposed to be as unpleasant as possible. But it won't be long before you're back on Mothers' Allowance, and that's not as bad."

"I'm fed up with Mothers' Allowance too. I've got to get a job."

Actually, Linda's whole problem was that she had just had a job. She had taken a local initiatives job. This meant that for six months she worked on a grant. She was now suffering the after employment blues. Her case of the blues was further complicated by the fact that there had been the usual foul-up at the provincial level, and they had really given her the treatment.

First her worker expressed delight that Linda had found a job, and said that she thought she could get Linda a lump sum of money. This turned out to be available only if Linda was getting a permanent job. Since this was LIP, Linda did not qualify. Then she said not to worry, Linda would still be covered for medical benefits by Mothers' Allowance. This was followed by a letter from the province, saying that since Linda was now working full-time, she was not eligible for medical coverage. A further letter stated that they had overpaid her, and she owed them a hundred and fifty dollars. Since LIP pays minimum wages, Linda was not exactly rolling in money, and she was very worried.

"We'll appeal," said Chiclet, and we drew up an appeal that was masterly. Of course, by this time Linda's job was over. One nice little facet of Mothers' Allowance is the fact that during an appeal, you cannot collect benefits. Oh, and of course her rent had gone up while she was working. It went down again after her job had finished, but at the end of six months, what had working done for her? Got her in trouble with Mothers' Allowance, that's what. And that's all. She was now on local Welfare, than which there is no more beastly fate.

Welfare has a little game it plays with its recipients. It's called Guess Who Has The Cheque. What they do is, they mail it out once or twice, so you get used to the idea that it comes by mail, and then one month it doesn't come. You figure it's in the mail, so you just borrow for a couple of days. Then you figure maybe they didn't mail it. You phone, and they tell you you have to go down and pick it up. A neat little twist here is that, no matter what end of town you live in, the cheque is in an office at the other end. They get extra points if you just got out of hospital. The next month, you figure you'll outsmart them, and you go down to get it, and they tell you it's in the mail.

I think their classic ploy is played at holiday time, though. I remember last Thanksgiving, Edna and her family were temporarily on Welfare, because her husband had been laid off. When the mail came Friday morning, there was no cheque. It was two days late, so Edna phoned to see if she had to go down.

"Oh, are you still on Welfare? When you didn't come

112

down for your cheque two days ago, we decided you didn't need it, and we sent it back. There's nothing we can do now, you know. It's a long weekend, and everybody's gone home."

I'm sure that this must be known as the McCoy Gambit, after her worker, and is now included in the handbook they give social workers.

Well, Edna had Thanksgiving dinner, because Chiclet went door-to-door, and rounded up the money. But if Edna hadn't been living in public housing, there would have been nothing to be thankful for that year.

Mothers' Allowance has different games, and the rules are easier to follow. Rule Number One is don't go to work. This was the rule Linda had broken. The only way to stay sane is to know what they really mean. For instance, when the Minister in charge of Mothers' Allowance makes a big public speech about how these lazy mothers should get off their behinds and work, HE DOESN'T MEAN IT. See, we're not listed officially as unemployed, so when we go to work, the unemployment rolls don't go down. Officially, they're always telling us to go to work, but unofficially, they make it far too uncomfortable and costly to do it. To keep your mind from taking a vacation, you have to learn to ignore all the official speeches. Really, what they're doing is paying you not to work, like paying farmers not to grow corn, only it's not popular politically, so they never pay you enough, and they make sure you don't enjoy it.

Once you know all this, living on Mothers' Allowance isn't too bad, and you can go along for a year without ever having to see your worker. This is a side benefit you don't enjoy on local Welfare.

Once you go to work, though, and get a taste of independence, you're ruined for Mothers' Allowance. It takes about a year before you can get back in the right frame of mind. But at that, it beats Unemployment

Insurance. I think the UIC workers have the Welfare handbook, and supplement it with special intensive lessons in How to be Insulting. But what were we going to do about Linda? Chiclet's answer to the ever-recurring employment problems is always the same. "We have to create the jobs. We know no one is going to hire us to do anything anybody else can do, so we have to come up with some new jobs."

"Chiclet, how? Not one of the new products we've invented have sold."

"Maybe that's the problem, Tillie. We were concentrating on making a new product, instead of *being* the product."

"I don't think that sounds very nice, Chiclet. It sounds like Harlots Anonymous."

"Well, maybe I put it wrong. Look Linda, Tillie, what is it that we're all good at?"

There was a blank pause here. I couldn't think of anything we were all good at. Mrs. Grocholski is a fantastic cook, but I can barely boil water. Chiclet can organize anything, but the rest of us can't. Mrs. Rotardier is a nurse, Linda is great at entertaining kids, Edna is a wonderful housekeeper, I write, and Poison Ivy can take anything back to a store. This is a real talent. She can take something that you've had for a year and never used, and have lost the sales slip for, and return it to a store you've never been to in your life, and they'll apologize for selling it.

"Chiclet, I can't think of anything we can all do, but there's lots of things we can do when you put them together."

"I think you're on the right track, Tillie. Like what?"

Linda said "We could throw children's parties. Lots of people don't have the time or the energy. Tillie, you could write a puppet play for those worms you made out of socks, and I could help put it on. Mrs. Grocholski could make the goodies, and Edna could get the place

114

ready, and we could help her tidy up after it. We could say something like 'Have your child's birthday party catered. No mess — no problems — you don't even have to be there! What do you think?"

"I like it."

"That's because you hate throwing parties, Tillie. It's good, but we only use a few people. Maybe it can be part of something bigger. Why don't we start a business called 'Ask your Next Door Neighbour.' Then we could do all sorts of things. We could feed people's goldfish when they're on vacation, or water their plants, or walk their dog, or visit their mother in the hospital, or take their kids to camp, or pick up their dry cleaning, or..."

"We could take their dog to the vet's."

"Right. That's horrible to do yourself."

"That's it. We'll do the dirty work."

"I can write nasty letters. Lots of people find that hard to do."

That is it. A new avenue to fame and fortune has opened up. We've decided not to apply for a grant this time. We'll form our own company. But none of us will go off Mothers' Allowance until we see how successful it is. There's still a lot of preliminary work to do, too. We don't know if we have to be bonded, and if we do, we don't know how. But we'll find out. One of our next door neighbours is checking that out, and another one is looking into finding a place we can work out of for nothing until we start to make some money because the Housing Authority won't let you operate a business on their premises, and another one is looking into how you get incorporated, and I'm writing up the ads.

I like the sound of this one. "You can trust us. We're your next door neighbours." Of course, we're not going to mention that we live in public housing.

THE DUMB LOOK

We were over visiting Edna, when the doorbell rang. We sat sipping our coffee waiting for her to come back, and fiddling with the tickets we were supposedly selling. Actually, whenever we went door-to-door in the project, we didn't get much selling done, or whatever it was we were trying to do, because we kept getting invited in for coffee and a chat. This was our eleventh cup of coffee, and it was only one o'clock. We were going to make an excuse and leave, when we heard voices coming down the hall, but then we saw Edna's face. She was wearing the Dumb Look. We settled back in our chairs.

If Edna was wearing the Dumb Look, it meant her visitors were official. Could be a public health nurse, social worker, or Housing Authority minion. Maybe this was why she wanted us to stay for coffee.

The Dumb Look could be called self-defence for minorities. It is worn by public housing tenants, blacks, Indians, French-Canadians, and children, at different times. Sometimes it's accompanied by an accent, or a shuffle, or a peculiar gesture. Chiclet and I hate the

116

Dumb Look, even though we know why it's necessary.

"Well, Mr. Prentiss. What a nice surprise."

"Hello, Ms. Gomez, Ms. Jamieson."

There was a slight pause while Mr. Prentiss waited for us to leave. We waited for Edna to give us some indication of whether she wanted us to stay, and sipped at our coffee.

"Are you making the rounds, Mr. Prentiss? I don't remember getting a notice, or I would have been at home."

"Oh, no. No, we just came to see a few people."

Hmm. What could he want with Edna? She wasn't breaking any rules. This makes her quite unusual, as most of us are breaking a few. With two whole pages of rules in small print included with the lease, this isn't surprising. But Edna is one of those people who stick to the letter of the law.

"Could Edna be using her plumbing for something it's not intended for?" This was one rule we found pretty funny, and we could spend hours thinking up things to do with our plumbing.

"Chiclet!" Edna went pink and started to laugh. It made the Dumb Look go away.

Mr. Prentiss went pink too, and began to shuffle.

"Uh, no, not at all, uh, the fact is, I just came to, uh, discuss, —"

Edna said politely "Yes?"

"I came to talk to you about moving."

"Moving? Did you ask for a transfer, Edna?"

"No."

I could see Edna was upset. Why would they want her to move? She had lived in this area of the city since she was a child, long before Urban Renewal had come along and displaced and then replaced her. Why would they want to displace her again?

"Your son has moved out, so you won't be wanting such a big place, so we came to ask if you would like to

117

move now, before your lease is up."

Aha! Of course! Why would Edna possibly need a four bedroom house any more, with only four children left in the house, conveniently divided into male and female, so that she could have two per bedroom? The girls were five and sixteen, and I happened to know that the sixteen year old had been rejoicing in the freedom of her own bedroom.

"Mr. Prentiss, we don't consider a child gone until they've made it on their own for a year. Even then, they may be back. Edna doesn't want to move."

Mr. Prentiss left, and Edna had a stay of execution. But we knew, unless we could figure something out, it was only temporary.

We could, of course, invite her son to come back home. But this would mean denying him the right and the responsibility he had just shouldered, and it would take privacy away from Edna's daughter. Obviously, what we had to do was come up with a bona fide reason why Edna still needed four bedrooms, even without her oldest son at home. Privacy for a teenage daughter was not enough.

We began to make some plans. This would call for a certain amount of scheming, so we called in the reserves. We weren't sure about calling in Poison Ivy, because we knew that she and Edna didn't really jell, but then Linda and Chiclet devised a plan.

When Ivy arrived, we told her we were going to have a party to celebrate Edna's transfer.

"How come Edna's getting a transfer?"

"She deserves it, Ivy. Edna's lived here ten years."

"So have I."

"Well, maybe you can have one next year. Anyway, we don't want you to say anything about Mary's problem, or Edna might not get her transfer."

"You know I never gossip. What problem?"

"Well, you know Mary's hyperactive. She should

118

have a room of her own, but if Edna gets a transfer, there won't be a four bedroom available. So we're not talking about it."

After Ivy left, Edna called Mary into the house, and told her to stay in. Mary is the five-year-old.

Sure enough, by about three o'clock there was a knock on the door and in came the public health nurse, Ms. Patterson.

"Well, Edna, what's this I hear about you moving?"

We were all wearing our Dumb Looks by this time. The reason we hate the Look is because it can get to be a habit, but in this case, it looked like a good idea.

"Well, Ms. Patterson, I think I can get a real nice three bedroom out in the other end of town."

"Edna, have you thought about the effect on the children?"

"Well.."

Here the nurse fixed Mary with a gimlet eye. Mary, aware that she was under scrutiny, and feeling cooped up because she hadn't been allowed out for a couple of hours, promptly began to fidget. Then, because she had a good audience, and because she genuinely wanted to go out and play, she went through the whole annoying list of things that five-year-olds do when they want their own way. She whined, she crawled all over Edna, and she climaxed her act by drumming her heels on the floor.

"Oh, for heaven's sake, Mary, go out and play," Edna said, as if she was getting rid of a burden.

"I'm sorry, Edna, I know you must have been counting on it, but I really think you should stay here in a four bedroom. Mary should have a room of her own, you know. The child is hyperactive."

"I think it's too late, Ms. Patterson. The Housing Authority is already making arrangements."

"Well, I'll take care of that."

With that, the nurse left. The poor woman was a

perfectly decent person, but we knew that we had to play it this way. If we had merely told her that Edna didn't want to leave because this was her home, and that Sheila was at the age where she needed a room of her own, she would have agreed that it was too bad, but she would not have been able to bring herself to protest. Under the impression, however, that Mary had a problem that none of the rest of us were able to recognize, she felt impelled to take action.

We weren't too worried about a follow-up on Mary, because we felt we could convince the nurse that a room of her own had, indeed, calmed Mary down, and no treatment would be necessary. We also had to remember to look properly downcast about the whole thing the next time we saw Ivy.

Then we all shuffled down to Chiclet's, and she broke out the dandelion wine she'd made two years before, that we had never dared to try. With good reason.

BETTER HOMES AND GARDENS

Chiclet was still in bed when there was a ring at her doorbell. Most people know that Chiclet is not at her best, to put it mildly, before 9:30, so we generally don't start bothering her until she's had time to get some coffee down her.

She figured it must be an emergency, so she hopped out in her nightie, and went to the window. "What?"

Under her window was a surprising sight.

"Tillie, I couldn't believe it. Every man in the project was down there, on my front lawn. Even the unofficial ones. On a Saturday morning. I just stood there with my mouth open."

"I know, Chiclet. They were at my house at eight. But don't knock it, I think it's great."

Earlier in the week, we had received a billet-doux from the Housing Authority. I had opened it with some trepidation, feeling that, as far as they're concerned, no news is good news. Sure enough, they had another pleasant little surprise for us. The word was out. Produce a nice looking lawn and garden, or pay a fine.

This sounds fairly straightforward, but there are a few

problems. For one thing, public housing is built either on solid rock or on a swamp. In one case, when you water the lawn, the water doesn't sink in, because what you have isn't a lawn, but a thin scattering of moss disguised as a lawn. In the other, unless you have a penchant for bulrushes, you might as well forget it. All a lawn serves to do over a swamp is disguise the treacherous spots. Besides these problems, when you have an area which is overrun by about five hundred children, without anywhere else to play, it is absurd to expect that the grounds will look as though all the inhabitants belong to a horticultural society. Of course, any lawn fronting a house with teenage males in it is also thoroughly saturated with crankcase oil and rust, as that is where they dismember engines. Any lawn with younger males is littered with go-cart wheels, boards, and nails.

In short, our project has that lived-in look.

When Chiclet received her letter, she stormed down to the Housing Authority. She went over the foregoing points, and ended up with her whammy. "How do you expect a single parent who works all day to have the energy, after work, and housecleaning, to attempt to fix up her garden?"

"Ms. Gomez, we are trying to get the tenants to take pride in their community. Now you know that we have offered to provide grass seed, flower seeds, and even fertilizer, so that the grounds will look nice. We have put trees, at our own expense."

Trees was not a good subject for Mr. Prentiss to have raised. We have never asked for trees. We have certainly not asked for two-hundred-and-fifty dollar trees. When we see them putting in trees we know that this means no paint for the inside of the houses. Besides that, this year we had had the great caterpillar invasion.

Chiclet had got a hysterical call from Linda. She has one weakness. Linda is great with blood, or fainting, or

122

anything medical, but she can't stand anything with more than four legs. "I phoned the Housing Authority, and they said call Maintenance. I called Maintenance, and they said call the Housing Authority. Chiclet, they're coming this way. Thousands of them. I'll cut it down. I'll get my little hatchet."

Chiclet had eventually dealt with the plague, and of course this meant the whole side of the project had to be dealt with. No point just asking the caterpillars to move next door.

Then, of course, it turned out that the trees produced poisonous berries. The Housing Authority's reaction to this had been beautiful in its simplicity. "Well, tell the children not to eat them."

This meant that every small tummy-ache sufferer got rushed to the hospital, or underwent the Inquisition for a simple surfeit of hot dogs.

Trees was definitely not a good subject for Prentiss to have brought up, although it did divert the mainstream of Chiclet's attack.

"They're not going to get away with this, Tillie. I'm not touching my lawn. Let them sue me."

Then the men of the community arrived.

"Ms. Gomez, we decided it wasn't fair on the single mothers to expect them to do their lawns. So we're doing them. Come on down and tell us what you want done. We're here to do it for you."

This put Chiclet in a dilemma. Mr. Prentiss had talked of teaching the tenants to take pride in our community. Of course, we do take pride in our community. It just doesn't come forth in the shape of lawns. We take pride in the people in our community, and in their caring for each other. So how could Chiclet refuse to have her lawn cared for by the men of our own community?

There was Poison Ivy's husband, hovering in the background, too shy to say anything, but ready to jeopardize his sure-fire win in the garden contest by fixing up other people's gardens. There was even Mr. Grocholski, brandishing the very rake Chiclet had lent him last year, which was originally mine, ready to be neighbourly. There was Charlie, our single parent male, refusing to claim special privilege. There was Edna's husband, Chicken Little, and Georgia's husband, and Linda's boyfriend.

How could Chiclet stand on principle when it would mean demolishing another principle? She couldn't.

"Tillie, I know how hard they work all week. I know how tired out they usually are. I couldn't say no. You take that side of the project, and I'll take this one. Get all the teenagers out to pick up the junk before they get there."

With a little urging, and a little moral blackmail, we soon had a squad of teenagers out picking up old tires and go-cart wheels. Then we got the little ones out collecting bottles. When we got enough Chiclet took them down to the store, and bought a couple of cases of beer. Georgia and Linda and I went door to door, rounding up food. When evening came, we had a lawn party. Georgia had some old Japanese lanterns, and we hung those up. The teens provided guitar music, and we even danced a little.

Chiclet flung herself down beside me, panting from the last whatever-it-was she'd just danced. "Prentiss may think he's won this one. But he hasn't. We did."

"Chiclet, don't the trees look nice with the Japanese lanterns in them?" I said. And ducked.

THE LONELY BLUES

"I'm getting married."

"What?"

"No!"

"Don't be an idiot!"

"You're kidding, aren't you?"

"Well," Linda said. "Isn't this nice? I come to my best friends to share my good news, and this is the reception I get."

"You took us by surprise," I said lamely. "Congratulations, Linda."

"You don't really mean that, Tillie. I can tell. You girls have never liked Bill, I know."

"Bill? You're going to marry Bill?"

"Well, who else?"

Almost anybody else, was my feeling, but I didn't voice it. I learned a long time ago that it doesn't do any good to criticize anybody else's kids, dogs, or husbands. It just makes them mad. And sometimes they'll do something stupid just to be stubborn. I had hopes that, if we left Linda alone for a while, she'd come to her senses.

"Why are you doing this, Linda? Why get married?"

125

"Why do people usually get married, Chiclet?"

"Stupidity, mostly."

This answer did not calm Linda down. She started spouting a lot of nonsense like this proved that he really loved her, and how good it would be for the children, and how she was tired of being alone. Well, she wasn't alone physically, because Bill had been living with her for a couple of months, but we knew what she meant. She was tired of having every single decision depend on her.

"What about Munroe, Linda? I thought he didn't like Bill."

"Munroe will learn to like him."

Munroe is a very stubborn ten-year-old. I figured he was about as likely to learn to like Bill as he was to learn to like homework.

"Is Bill going to learn to like Munroe? Does he ever go to visit his own kids? I never even hear him mention them."

"That's different. He can't stand their mother."

"Chiclet, leave her alone. When's the wedding, Linda?"

"It won't be until next year. I still have to get my divorce, and Bill has to get his. We were thinking of getting married in October. And Bill has to get a job, of course."

Oh well then. A year gave her lots of time to change her mind, and if it depended on Bill getting a job....

During the next few weeks we got very used to hearing the phrase "Bill says." "Bill says the government is full of crooks." "Bill says all the good jobs go to Frenchmen." "Bill says the unions just rip you off." We got very sick of Bill and his pronouncements. But we were cheered up by what they meant. They meant he hadn't got a job.

Munroe began spending more and more time over at Chiclet's. When Chiclet tried to discuss it with Linda, all

126

she got was more "Bill says". "Bill says Munroe has got to learn to accept authority."

"I hate him," Munroe whispered to Chiclet one day. "I hate his guts. He says I never do anything right. He wants Mom to send me to live with my father."

"Do you want to go, Munroe?"

Munroe just shrugged.

Then Linda asked Chiclet not to let Munroe come over any more.

"It's not good for him, Chiclet. He's just running away. You can't run away from life."

"Bill says," murmured Chiclet.

"What?"

"Look, Linda. Munroe's going through a bad time right now. He thinks Bill doesn't like him. He thinks you don't like him any more. If I tell him he can't come back, he's going to think I don't like him either. Do you really want a ten-year-old to think nobody likes him?"

"I'm sorry, Chiclet. Ordinarily I think you're usually right, but this is my business. I mean it Chiclet. I don't want Munroe over here. Or at your place either, Tillie."

Well, what could we do? To let him come anyway would just be to get him in more trouble, and end up with nobody speaking to anybody.

About five days later, Munroe ran away. Linda came over with blood in her eye, and accused Chiclet of hiding him.

"I don't have him, Linda. But I wish I did. I really don't know where he is."

The police brought him back that night, and he ran away again the next day. They brought him back, and he ran away. Bill began to talk loudly of sending Munroe away to a Training School, because he was "incorrigible".

The next time I saw Linda, she looked as if she'd been crying, but when I walked over toward her in the store, she moved away. I decided that I was probably blacklisted, and if I was, Chiclet would be too.

"Well, I guess we're not going to get to be bridesmaids, Chiclet."

"Tillie, I don't know what we can do. But if she doesn't smarten up, something awful's going to happen. It's not just Munroe. Melody's having a hard time too." Melody is a cheery, bouncy little four-year-old. The thought of somebody taking all the bounce out of her was depressing.

Linda came over the next day. "Can I come in, Chiclet?"

"You have to ask?"

"I've been a real fool, Chiclet."

"Where did you get the black eye?"

"Bill. But it was cheap at the price. He's gone. He's not coming back into my house ever again. I don't know what's wrong with me. I must be a real idiot, letting that stupid lump tell me who I can talk to, and who my kids can talk to, and scolding them for every little thing. I just hope my kids aren't permanently damaged."

"Well, not as badly as they would be if you'd married him. What was the last straw?"

"Oh, he spanked Melody for spilling her milk. But it wasn't just that. She's scared of him, and she was never scared of anybody in her life before. That made me mad, and I was going to come over here and talk and pull myself together, and he forbade me. So I said 'You don't own me, Bill', and that's when I really realized he figured he did. I wanted to get out of the wedding a week ago, but I didn't know how."

"Well, you're out now."

"Chiclet, if I ever do anything that stupid again, or look as if I'm going to, give me a swift kick, will you?"

Well, Linda's kids look okay again, and Munroe is really trying to be the man of the house.

The trouble is none of us are immune. We can all get really stupid when the lonelies hit us. Love isn't as blind as loneliness can be.

128

THE GRANT GAME

Did you ever see the card trick we used to do as kids, where out of the whole deck you convince someone that they picked the card you had in mind? It makes them believe in ESP. The way you do it is, if they pick red and you want them to pick red, you throw away the black; but if they pick black and you want them to pick red, you still throw away the black. If you're fast enough, they think they're doing it themselves.

Government has a trick just like this – it's called citizen participation. It took a long time for Chiclet and me to catch on, but eventually we got to see the trick being played.

We'd go to a meeting, and say we wanted better housing. They'd say "Great! Join the citizens' committee." We'd sit on this committee a couple of years, and when we picked red, they'd throw away the black, and when we picked black, they'd still throw away the black. Then we'd sit back and look at the new houses, which look exactly the same as the old houses do, and we'd say to each other "Strange. Why did we pick that? Government must know what we want, after all."

Then we caught on.

"It's a sucker's game, Chiclet. The house always wins. Government is just a big shell game. You can't break the bank – you just get a new dealer."

"There must be a system, Tillie."

Chiclet is a born gambler. After a while, she thought she had it figured out. We would try to get around the government through grants.

So, for a couple of years, we've lived on grants. LIP grants, OFY grants, Canada Works grants. I sure know how to write up a grant application now, even if I don't know much else.

Rule Number One: Never tell them what you're actually going to do. Pick a fancy name that doesn't mean anything.

Rule Number Two: Ask for three times the number of people you want, and you may get half the number you want.

Rule Number Three: Ask for three times the amount of money you need, and you may get almost enough.

Rule Number Four: Halfway through the grant, start planning the next one.

If you follow all these rules, you'll end up working your head off for nothing, and swearing you'll never do it again. But you will. It gets in your blood. Even though there's no security, and the pay is lousy, there's something about planning the work you'll be doing that makes anything else look tame by comparison. Of course if the type of job you would otherwise get is working in a bra factory, it's twice as attractive.

In the last little while, Chiclet and Linda and I have done all kinds of worthwhile work in the community through grants. But our favourite schemes never did get approved.

One of these was a dating bureau for our women. Lots of our people never get to go anywhere, like the show, or to a play, or to a nightclub. Some of our people haven't been out to dinner in years. That's not healthy.

So we got a grant application, and began to follow the rules. First, the name.

"How about 'Fun Anonymous'?"

"Linda, the secret is you never let on what you're going to do. We need something less definite. What do you think, Chiclet?"

"Ladies and Escorts."

"Be serious. How about 'Project Self-Expression'?"

"All right. Now how do we cover up what we're going to do?" Linda catches on quickly.

The problem was, what *were* we going to do? We didn't know where to go to look for men. We would hold a dance, and seventy-five women and three men would turn up. Pretty soon, the women would start to leave, murmuring something about baby-sitters, and that would be that.

Chiclet might be employed, we thought, to teach women her style. When she goes to a dance like that, she picks out a target, moves in, and yells "You! Let's dance!" Either she gets a dance, or she doesn't. It works out about fifty-fifty. But she never just sits along the wall like the shy ones do, never getting to dance. But if we did that, we wouldn't be helping that many women, and Chiclet could hardly spend six months going to dances.

"What about soldiers? We could write one of the army camps, and ask them to send down a busload."

"I don't know, Linda — that seems too easy. And it's a little crass. Besides, all the soldiers I've seen lately look about eighteen. We want men."

"What about when we had the riot, and there were all those policemen?"

"Chiclet, I'm not going to get involved in a riot so I can get a date. Besides, they were all married. It's an occupational hazard. But what about Mounties? Remember that protest we went on, and around the back of the building there were a whole bunch of them in a bus?"

Thoughts of attending a protest to highjack a busload of Mounties were reluctantly discarded. Someone would be sure to miss them.

Nuts. Where could we take our clients to meet men? According to Dear Abby and other columns, if you hang around churches and community centres you can meet some, but the community centres are full of women making flowers out of Kleenex, and the only single men I've ever seen in a church were taking holy orders.

We looked in the personal ads. They were full of blurbs like "Intelligent woman with many interests seeks male companionship for theatres, skiing, ballet, etc.". It doesn't say who pays. How do you put that in the ad without being crass?

We designed an ad. It said "Good-natured welfare recipient going crazy at home with only junior companionship. Help wanted, male." We decided it wouldn't do. For one thing, it was too honest, and for another, it sounded too much like we wanted husbands, and that's the last thing we wanted.

Contrary to propaganda, it's men who want to get married. Every year, they come out with some study that shows married men live longer, and have fewer health problems than single men; but married women are in more trouble than single women. Most of our women know this, and remarriage is considered a last resort, if all else fails.

Then we thought we might run a television show, with a different client as the feature each week. We could call it "Would you date this woman?"

"This is Chiclet. She is twenty-eight years old. She has three children. Two of them do Monty Python imitations, and the other one isn't housebroken. She would like someone to take her bowling. Are you man enough to try?" Or: "This is Linda. She has two children. She likes movies. Her ex-husband has threatened to strangle anyone he sees going out with her..." No.

The last time Linda went out with someone, she met him a couple of miles away, and left him in the same place, but when she came home, her ex was there, waiting for her. He had sent the babysitter home, and was threatening to take the kids from her. Chiclet sent Bruno over to throw him out, and then we had a meeting. How did he know? Was the house bugged? We began wandering around, peering behind the fridge, trying to sound innocuous.

Chiclet picked up a lamp, and began to take it apart. "Well, Linda, I guess you'll just have to stay home." Nothing there.

"Chiclet's right, Linda." I turned the table over. Nothing but gum on the bottom. Then I realized something. I didn't know what a bug looked like. I gestured to Chiclet and Linda, and we all went into the bathroom. Chiclet lifted up the ball in the tank, and the toilet kept flushing.

"What does it look like? Chiclet?"

"Well, it's small, and black. Maybe it has wires. Do you know, Linda?"

"I think they run on batteries, and they stick to things."

Chiclet thought we might be able to spot a bug with feedback, so we borrowed a hearing aid from a friend and walked around with it on, trying to get something to beep at us. Then we tried a walkie-talkie belonging to one of Linda's kids. Nothing. After we finally gave up, we were up until about three in the morning, putting lamps back together, and legs on tables, pushing the stove back against the wall, and trying to get the toilet to stop flushing.

We obviously couldn't advertize Linda, and probably

a lot of the other women would find it awkward too.

We were still looking for some tasteful way to advertize when we realized we'd missed the closing day for applications. It was too bad, too. We were sure we could have disguised what we were going to do once we figured it out. We know all about applying for grants. You just throw away the black...

BRUNO

The first thing you have to learn to live with in public housing is the fact that the neighbours know everything you're doing. The second thing you have to learn to live with is that they don't care. The first takes about six months to get used to, and the second some never manage.

Except for the odd tenant like Poison Ivy, who can't find anything more exciting to do, however, we really don't care what the neighbours are doing, as long as it's not a danger to the community as a whole. When I say the neighbours don't care, I mean that they're not making judgements — certainly if you need help, you'll get it. But if you don't want any help, people will pretend they don't notice.

We have one man in the community who we all count on for support. We don't ask him to fix cars, or move furniture, because we save him for desperate measures. Desperate measures include repelling unpleasant ex-husbands and ex-boyfriends, and dealing with teen age boys who start to feel their oats. When an emergency happens the call goes out "Get Bruno."

Bruno is about six foot three, and built like an old west cowboy, with broad shoulders and hardly any hips at all. He drives a taxi, when he's working. He only works about half the year. Bruno lives with the Rotardiers. Nobody seems to know why, or why he only works half the year, or what he's always reading when he gets a call. Even Poison Ivy doesn't know, although she's made a lot of guesses. Bruno is sort of brown, but his eyes are bright blue. He doesn't seem to smoke, or drink, or swear, or fool around that we have ever seen. Sometimes he does play the guitar, but only soft ballads.

He is always perfectly willing to drop everything and help. When Georgia went to the hospital to have her last kid, it was Bruno who drove her, because her husband was out of town, and Bruno who waited to hear what she had, and brought us back the news. When Linda Cunningham's ex turned up, looking for trouble, it was Bruno who told him quietly to get lost. When some kid at school started leaning on one of Chiclet's kids, it was Bruno who walked him to school the next day. Chiclet would have gone herself, of course but her kid didn't want to bring his mother, he wanted to walk with a big male. Bruno is sort of a Community Resource.

So when we began to suspect that something was bothering Bruno, we all were concerned. We didn't want to intrude on his privacy by asking what was wrong, so we did a lot of speculating. First we thought maybe we were asking him to do too many things, so we tried to cut down on our requests. This didn't seem to help. Then we thought maybe the Housing Authority had found out he was living with Rotardiers, so we worked out a system where Bruno could "visit" a different family every month, and we could keep him in the community. When we delicately approached Mrs. Rotardier with our plan, she said she wasn't having any trouble about keeping him, and she was worried, too, but she didn't know what was bothering him.

We decided we would have to take the bull by the horns, and somebody would have to ask Bruno what was bothering him. But who? We generally nominate people who aren't at a meeting for anything the rest of us don't want to do, but Poison Ivy was the only regular missing, and we didn't want to appoint her. I finally said I would do it, although I didn't want to, because Bruno was a lot younger than me, and I didn't know him very well. The others said this was perfect.

So the next time I saw Bruno out on the step, strumming his guitar, I went over and worked my way between admiring teenage girls until I managed to sit down beside him.

"Hi Bruno."

"Hello, Tillie. Trouble?"

"No, no. I just thought I'd wander over and keep you company. How are things going?"

"Fine."

"Working?"

"No."

I couldn't think of anything else to ask, so I just sat there while Bruno played requests from the gallery. Finally I got up to go.

"Don't go, Tillie. Come on in and have a cup of tea."

I had never been in the Rotardiers' kitchen before, but all these places are built alike, and I had no trouble finding the tea, and making it. Bruno was still fiddling with his guitar.

"Where do you come from, Tillie?"

"I was born on the prairies, Bruno. Why, where do you come from?"

"I don't know. I don't know who my parents were, or anything about them. I don't know what I am. I grew up in foster homes. Tillie, I'm going to have to leave here. I want to know who I am, and what my background is."

"Why?"

"Someday, I'll want to get married, and have kids of my own, and what can I tell them when they ask what they are?"

"Bruno, you're very important to us. We love you. We could be your family. We need you."

It was no use. His mind was made-up. He was bound to go.

"Where will you start?"

"I'll go back to my last foster home, and see if they can tell me about my placement, and follow it back."

"You might be Italian, Bruno. Or Portuguese. Or maybe West Indian, or East Indian. How will it help to know? Do you speak Italian?

"Tillie, I know it doesn't make sense. But I have to know."

"When are you leaving?"

"On the weekend."

I went back and informed the committee of what I had found out. We decided to throw a big party in the back. The party's high point was when we sold lottery tickets on Bruno's background. The rules were, when he came back, the prize would go to whoever bought the right ticket. If he was a mixture, the prize would be divided among the people who held those tickets. We decided to put the prize money in the bank to collect interest, and gave the rest to Bruno for travelling money. He kissed all of us good bye, even Poison Ivy, and there wasn't a dry eye to be seen.

He's promised to come back when he finds his heritage, and we're counting on it. We keep the older teens in line with "when Bruno comes back" and make believe to troublesome ex-husbands that he's just at the store.

I hope he gets back soon, although I'm not too happy with my ticket. I don't think I stand a chance. It says "Ukrainian" but there are those bright blue eyes.

THE POTBELLY PILFERER, or THE HEIST AT THE CO-OP

Public housing — that name has always made me feel exposed — like our houses were flophouses or something. It has that effect on members of the general public, too. They feel, it seems, as if anything called public housing should be open to the public. So teenagers especially come into our areas when they're going to do something they can't get away with anywhere else. You can pass strangers' cars in our parking lots where somebody's smoking marijuana or drinking beer and throwing the bottles on our lawns. If we object, they point out that the houses don't belong to us. Well, the Prime Minister's house doesn't belong to him either, but I don't see anybody smoking up in his driveway.

However, we get to know each other and each other's visitors pretty well so when there are out-and-out strangers in the community, we know it. We just aren't sure what to do about it.

Edna hates strangers in the community. She particularly hates the ones who come in, burn rubber, screech tires, then turn around and roar out again. She tried going the usual route and complaining to various people, like the police and the Housing Authority. Nothing happened. She took up a petition to get speed bumps erected, but the reaction from the Housing Authority was that we couldn't have them because they would "ruin the cars". This was not a popular decision with us. So Edna took matters into her own hands. She is the pitcher for the women's baseball team, and has developed her pitching arm to some degree. Now when cars roar into the parking lots, endangering the smaller children, Edna pitches a bottle directly in front of the car. She follows it up with a warning that next time it will be the windshield. This seems to be having some effect.

But we still keep a weather eye out for strangers. Of course, our trained eyes recognize minions of the Housing Authorities or social workers the minute they come in, and we know what they're up to, so we don't worry. But we always keep an eye on any other kind of stranger.

They had a worrisome stranger in Portobello Towers the other night. The tenants in Potbelly spotted him as he entered the front door of the larger building. Most of Potbelly's tenants are handicapped, and so they tend to be a little nervous. Chiclet got a call, and we hurried out there. Potbelly has a little food co-operative and snack bar in the larger building, Tower A, and the feeling was that the stranger was probably going to rob it.

By the time we got there, he had been in the co-op twice without buying anything, and the woman in charge, Freda Foley, was nearly hysterical.

"Where is he now, Freda?"

"I don't know. He took the elevator. He's probably still in the building. Oh, Chiclet, Mike is due to come down in a few minutes and pick up the cash box. What if he runs into him?"

"No robber is going to bother Mike until after he picks up the cash, Freda. He'll be all right."

140

Mike is Freda's husband. He's blind.

Chiclet began to organize. She went to the lobby and began to push buttons for various floors. "Mr. Laframboise? Chiclet Gomez. Could you go down to the elevator with a couple of other people on your floor, and sort of sit there chatting? Use your wheelchair to block it off, sort of accidentally, would you? There's a stranger in the building. Thanks."

Within a few minutes, she had organized Tower A so that if he got off the elevator, or on, on any floor, word would be transmitted to the lobby right away. She got some of the kids playing in the stairwell, something they are normally forbidden to do, so they were quite happy to co-operate.

Everyone knew they were not to try to stop him, merely to keep track of him.

Tower B connects to Tower A through the garage underground, so she headed over there to spread the word, and get the watchers organized. In the meanwhile I manned the lobby, trying to look inconspicuous, as if I was merely looking for the name of some relative.

Mervyn Perkins turned up. Mervyn is one of our teenagers who's always into something. He's caused us a few headaches in the past, but when it comes to securing the building against outsiders, we can count on him.

"Tillie, how about if I go down to the garage and pretend I'm working on my car? Then if he turns up there, I can sort of follow him."

Too late. He was gone. All I could do was hope that he had his own car, and was not going to dismantle some neighbour's car in the interests of criminal investigation.

Chiclet came back and reported Tower B secure. There had been no word on the intercom about where our wandering suspect had got to. At this point, I wanted to call the police, but Chiclet pointed out that the suspect had so far done nothing criminal, and could

141

yet turn out to be a visitor, although his visits to the co-op certainly looked suspicious. Still, he could be a dutiful son visiting a parent, and looking for something to tempt her appetite.

This was beginning to remind me of the story of the mice who wanted to bell the cat. If we caught him, what would we do with him? Also, it was beginning to get pretty late, and surely the sight of all these people still up and roaming the halls when it was going on eleven o'clock would make him suspicious, if he wasn't already.

"Chiclet, can't we phone the police, and just ask them to sort of lurk outside, and then if he does something, we can signal them with a flashlight or something?"

"One if by land, two if by sea?"

"Well, why not? We could give two blinks if he's coming out through the lobby, and three if he's coming out through the garage."

"Chiclet?" The voice came through the intercom, "this is Mabel on seventeen. He just took the elevator."

Instantly, Chiclet was galvanized into action, and began contacting people on the various floors. A report came in from fifteen. Mike, who was to pick up the cash, had got on the elevator with the stranger. When the elevator got to the ground floor, Chiclet and I were watching as the stranger and Mike both got off and headed for the co-op, and we trailed along behind, trying to look inconspicuous.

I kept wondering what on earth we would do with him until the police were called. Mike got to the floor of the co-op, now closed, and gave the knock. The door opened, and Mike walked in, the stranger slipping in behind him. As the door started to close, Chiclet began to run, and I pounded along after her. Just before the door closed and locked, Chiclet gave a kick, and the door exploded inward once again.

Freda shrieked. "He has a knife!"

142

I slowed down, but Chiclet speeded up. "The place is surrounded," she yelled. It was, by this time, but not by police. By wheelchairs.

I entered the room just in time to see him vanish through the stairway door. I heard shrieks of "He's headed for the garage," from the kids still playing there.

"Someone get Tower B and warn them," yelled Chiclet as she headed down the stairway in a headlong rush.

I reversed myself, and picked my way through the wheelchairs, back to the lobby. I warned Tower B to be on the lookout, and ran to the elevator.

When I got to the basement, it was full of people. The police were there, and they had our bandit, and everybody seemed to be talking at once.

When there was a quiet moment, I seized it. "Who called you?" I asked the large constable standing within earshot. "I thought nobody was going to call you until we found out for sure if it was a robbery."

"We weren't called for a robbery, ma'am. We were called for an attempted car theft." He nodded toward Mervyn Perkins.

"Mervyn!"

"I wasn't stealing it, I was fixing it."

We explained to a somewhat sceptical pair of policemen Mervyn's idea about keeping an eye open in the garage. I was worried.

"Excuse me," someone said from behind me, "that's my car, and I called the police when I saw this kid fooling around under the hood. What do you mean you fixed it?"

"You had a knock in the engine," said Mervyn, "and it's gone now. Try it."

Chiclet and I eventually got home about 2 a.m. The robber was being charged, and Mervyn had proved helpful, rather than harmful.

"I told you we should have called the police" I said,

"what would we have done with him if they weren't there?"

"Oh, Tillie, what if he'd turned out to be a legitimate visitor, like the other one?"

The other one! What was the owner of the car doing there?

"Oh, Tillie! We forgot to take Tower B off alert."

I just snarled, and went in and to bed. So did Chiclet.

A PERFECT STRANGER

Have you ever felt like murdering a perfect stranger? Well, he certainly wasn't perfect, but stranger describes him pretty accurately. He was stranger, all right.

I have often in the past amused myself with imaginary vengeance on Fat Freddy and King Kong. Pretty juvenile, I suppose, but very satisfying. Boiling in oil is one of my favourites. But usually they are the only ones I feel this way about. Well, except that one time we found out about this peculiar life insurance policy both King Kong and Mr. Grocholski carried. It seems they paid double if you got hit by a bus or a taxi. We played around with that one for a while, but we couldn't figure out how to get them together since they hated each other much less how to find a homicidal taxi driver.

But this was serious. We all hated Powell Parnell, the local hot-shot radio announcer. Public housing tenants all over the city hated Powell Parnell. Welfare recipients all over the city hated Powell Parnell. As far as we knew, none of us had even laid eyes on him, but we had heard him every day on his poisonous phone-in programme. The hatred was reciprocal. He hated us and all he figured we stood for.

Actually, what we stood for was hard to say. But what we wouldn't stand for was easy. We wouldn't stand for any more of Powell Parnell. But what to do?

Georgia Wiseman wanted to invite him over to meet us. She figured once he got a load of her, he wouldn't keep spouting all this poison about freeloaders and parasites. A few other people who figure to know us is automatically to love us agreed. Chiclet and I figured a hatred that well-developed wouldn't be easy to shake. We wanted to know why he hated us.

The meeting that we had about Powell Parnell attracted about a hundred women from the different projects, and a sprinkling of men. It was by far the best attendance we'd ever had for any meeting.

Suggestions from the floor were debated. Those dealing with homicide were tabled until later. First, we'd try peaceful means.

The most popular idea was for Chiclet to write him a letter, and challenge him to a debate on his radio show. I didn't like this one. After all, it was his radio show. I figured if he looked like he was losing, he could always switch to a commercial, and hope Chiclet lost track of what she was saying.

I favoured having all of us phone in during his phone-in show every day for a week, saying that he didn't know what he was talking about, no matter what subject he picked. I would have been willing to do all the phoning myself, but I figured it would lose its impact if it was always the same voice.

The trouble with Parnell was that his show seemed to attract all the real buggies out of the woodwork. People would phone his show with horrifying stories about Welfare recipients they had known, or heard of. These stories made Lizzie Borden look like a nice, all-round girl. They made Allo-Polis look like a comic book. After a half hour of his programme, you felt like

Typhoid Mary, Jack the Ripper, the Marquis de Sade, and Lucrezia Borgia had all been public housing tenants. Actually, with the exception of Typhoid Mary, they were all rich, but do you ever hear that mentioned?

The final vote was a combination of the two plans. First, we would inundate his show with phone calls pro us, and we would wind up the week with the challenge. We decided to make the challenge on the air, so he couldn't just ignore it. We wanted to start off with famous public housing tenants, but we only had two. One was Chiclet, and the other was a kid from another project who had risked his life on the ice to save his puppy. We decided to start off with him. We all memorized his name, and the name of his puppy, so we would have the facts right. That's the first rule in a good public fight. Always have your facts straight. We decided to save Chiclet for the end of the week.

By halfway through the week, I was wondering whether we wouldn't have been better off ignoring the whole thing. Reaction to our phone-in had been fairly mixed. Along with a few genuine phoners who thought Jimmy Chin was pretty brave, there had been an assortment of weirdies who wanted to know how his family could afford to keep a dog, whether the dog was licensed, whether there wasn't a plot on our part to inundate the city with pregnant mongrels, whether the dog hadn't in fact saved him, and whether either of them were worth it. There had also been one threat of dognapping.

If this was the reaction to our hero, what was going to be the reaction to Chiclet Gomez, part French, part Irish, part Mexican, and wholly Canadian public housing tenant? I shuddered to think.

I also shuddered to think of Chiclet's reaction. The trouble was, she not only reacted to anti-public housing or anti-poor propaganda, she reacted to anti-Catholic, anti-French, anti-Irish, and just about any other anti-you

147

could think of. If she met somebody who was anti-French, she would immediately be French, even though her French is, to say the least, limited. Her Catholicism is limited, too, but it sprang out in full feather if somebody slighted it. I was just waiting for her to start saying Begorrah to anyone even vaguely anti-Irish. She was also fully capable of claiming to be East Indian, Chinese, Black, Canadian Indian, or anything else that looked discriminated against. After all, she kept saying, in this country nobody knows for sure. Who knows what some great-grandmother might have been up to?

It looked like our side might get slaughtered. Everybody began to give Chiclet advice about what to say, even before we got the challenge on the air. Most of it conflicted with the advice of the person immediately prior. I kept trying to tell Chiclet to be ladylike, and not lose her temper. Linda kept saying "Give him Hell, Chiclet", and Georgia told her to keep her voice low and sexy.

Finally, late into the show Friday, Chiclet got on and produced her challenge. After a brief pause, Parnell invited her to come on the show Monday, and they would spend half the show debating, and the other half taking phone calls.

We spent all weekend trying to figure out what she should wear. Since this was a radio programme, this was a little silly, but we wanted to get to Parnell psychologically, too. Georgia brought over an extremely low-cut gown and a blond wig. I favoured a tailored suit effect. There was a pile of clothing, make-up, hair, and shoes on the couch when Chiclet made her announcement.

"I'm going just the way I always go."

So she did. Pigtails, sneakers, jeans and all. I figured she was right. After all, half the battle on a radio show is to be comfortable.

We sat down to listen. The show started off rough, and it stayed pretty rough. Chiclet admitted that she lived on Welfare. She admitted that her rent was subsidized. She admitted that she had never held down a paying job for over six months. Then she got in a few points. He admitted getting a loan from CMHC to help pay for his house. He admitted that his education had been subsidized by the rest of us, just like everybody else's. Then Chiclet got in about how hydro is subsidized, and health, and roads, and water, and the National Arts Centre, and bus fare, and air fare, and all that. He had to admit it.

Then he asked her if she was married. When he found out she was a single parent, he let another side of his charming personality show, and started in on her sex life. So then she found out that he was separated too, and started asking whether he paid his wife any support, or if he was one of those rotters who just walked out.

Aha! Out it came. He figured he paid too much support and his wife was a leech. Chiclet countered with all the women in public housing who get no support at all, except from the city.

At the half-way point, it was a tie. Chiclet was holding her own, even though he had started in on Women's Lib after exhausting the other subjects.

I raced for the phone. So did the rest of us. Too late. Some of them must have been waiting for hours there were so many people ahead of us. Most of them were anti-us. For one thing, everyone who had ever gone to university, or taken a loan from CMHC furiously resented being compared to us. Men callers resented remarks about running out on responsibility. Women callers resented Chiclet speaking for them. Some callers resented what other callers had just said. Some callers wanted to know what happened to the puppy everyone was discussing last week. Others wanted to yell about the government being too socialist, and feeding parasites like Chiclet. Some wanted to know if she practiced birth control, and whether all her kids had the same father, and if so, where was he?

I was so mad at not getting the line, and at what all the other callers were saying, I hardly heard what Chiclet answered. I was so mad I was jumping up and down. I kept dialling. Finally Linda came running in, and said they weren't taking any more calls. I hung up the phone, and I heard Parnell invite Chiclet back the next day.

She said "I've got a better idea. Why don't you come down to the project and have lunch next week? Then we'll debate on my ground."

So he's coming. We asked Chiclet what he looks like, so we'll recognize him, but she says he just looks like everyone else.

But I figure we'll know when we see him. The word is out. No tripping, eggs or tomatoes. After all, he didn't cut to a commercial in the middle of Chiclet's answers, so we're determined to be just as fair.

First we're going to feed him in the Community Centre, and then we're going to get him. But we're going to be civilized about it. We won't even ask about his sex life.